Kringle

A Fairy Tale

By Nosh Tims

December 24/2003
Vancouver, BC

"Twas the night before Christmas and all through the house, not-"

"Daddy?" Taylor asked, looking up at her father.

Joe was sitting on the edge of the little girl's bed, book open on his lap. He sighed softly and closed the cover of the Christmas story. He knew his daughter well and one question meant two, and two meant ten. No more reading would be happening this night before Christmas. "Yes, Tazie," he replied, ever so reluctantly.

"What's that all over the window?"

Taylor was eight years old, an age when everything was still relatively new and interesting. Sometimes Joe longed for those days, when there was still mystery in the world. "What, baby? Do you mean the frost?"

"Yeah," She responded. She was tucked into bed with her pillows propped up under her head and her favorite reindeer pajamas on. Her blond hair was pulled into two tight pony tails, something Taylor's mother insisted on doing every night before sleep. Joe could never understand why. Okay, so maybe there were still a *few* mysteries left after all. "But why is it all jagged?" she continued. "It looks like a spider web."

"Because it's jack frost," Joe told her.

3

"Jack Frost? Who's he?"

"Well," Joe began, quickly sifting through his mind in an attempt to find an adequate answer so that they might be able continue with the story book. Reading required much less thinking on his part. "He is winter, I guess. If he looks in through a window, his breath freezes it that way."

"Really," Taylor gasped, sounding equally nervous and excited by the idea. "What's he looking for?"

Trying to keep things anchored on the big day that was coming tomorrow morning, he said, "He's looking for Santa Claus."

"Oh!" Taylor thought about this for a moment before asking, "Why? Are they friends?"

"No," Joe replied hesitantly. "Not really. It's kind of a long story Tazie. I thought you wanted to hear 'Twas a Night Before Christmas?"

"Why is he called Santa Claus?" she now asked, seamlessly averting his bid to return to the story.

"He's called a lot of different things," Joe said, graciously accepting his defeat. "Some cultures call him Santa Claus, some call him Saint Nicholas. I think he's called Sinterklaas in Finland. Also Kris Kringle. That's the name I like best."

"Kris Kringle?" She replied, followed by more pondering. "Why does he visit kids in the winter? Why not in the summertime when it's nicer outside?"

"He lives in the North Pole, so I guess he likes the cold."

"Has he always lived in the North pole?"

"Not always, but for a very, very long time."

"Oh......So how does he know who's naughty or nice?"

Wow, Joe thought, *these questions are getting tougher by the second*. "Umm.....I suppose he can just tell. In his heart." Joe looked at his daughter then and saw the apprehension in her face. Something was on her mind. "Why all the questions about Santa, babe?" he asked.

Taylor looked at him with eyes that were on the verge of tears. "Some kids at school say that he's not real," she blurted out. "They say that the parents buy the presents and put his name on them. They say that only babies believe in Santa Claus."

They sure talk a lot, don't **they,** Joe thought. *Well this just will not do. I'm not ready for my baby girl to stop believing in Santa. Not yet. This needs to be nipped*. "Are these the same kids that read Harry Potter and all that wizard stuff?" He asked her.

Taylor nodded slowly.

"So they figure that believing in wizards is ok, but not Santa?"

His daughter shrugged.

"Well, you know that Santa doesn't visit kids that don't believe in him, right?" he asked, keeping his tone casual.

5

"I didn't say that I don't believe in him," Taylor stated quickly. "But the whole thing does seem a little far-fetched."

"Far-fetched?" Joe repeated with surprise. *Kids are growing up so fast these days.*

"Yeah. I mean, flying reindeer? Reindeer don't have wings or jet packs so how do they fly? And how does Santa fit down the chimney? He is kinda chubby. And how does his sleigh hold enough toys to give to every kid in the whole world? And how--"

"Hold on, hold on," Joe said, holding up his hands. "I get your point." He put the story book onto her bedside table. "Obviously there are things about Santa that are difficult to explain. But that's what's so fun about him, isn't it? The magic and mystery?"

Taylor shrugged again. "But usually if something can't be explained, then that means it's not true," she said.

Joe's eyes widened. *Where does this kid get her brains*, he wondered. "Not all the time," he replied finally. "And I didn't say they couldn't be explained, I said they were *difficult* to explain."

Taylor looked at her father with doubtful eyes.

"Ok," Joe sighed. "I'll tell you what. If you get all tucked in there under the covers, and promise me you'll go right to sleep afterwards, I'll tell you a story."

Taylor's face filled with excitement. "About Santa?"

"Sort of," he told her. "But it's about a lot of others things too. Including wizards."

"Cool," Taylor exclaimed as she snuggled under the covers.

Joe nodded. "In fact, there was a war between all the wizards that lived."

"A war," she breathed. "They were fighting with each other?"

Joe nodded again. "Yup. For many, many years. In the end, there was only one wizard left."

Taylor's eyes were wide. "Wow."

"But let's not get ahead of ourselves," Joe said. "Let's start this story right. Let's start it how all good stories should start. Do you know the words, Tazie?"

Taylor nodded her head excitedly.

"Ok, then go ahead and say them, nice and loud."

Taylor sat up and cleared her throat. Then, in her most important sounding voice, she said...

Noel Kringle

Once upon a time, a long, long time ago, the world beneath our feet was a very different place. The continents that are now scattered over the face of our planet were not yet divided by oceans. There was, at this time, only one land rising out of the surging waters that covered the rest of the world.

And this lone land, at the beginning, was a harsh and unforgiving place. A never ending winter of snow and ice blanketed every hill and valley from the Great Mountains to the ocean. Snow and sleet poured down from the sky for most of the year. It was truly a special day when the sun would peek out from behind a gray cloud. But even on those rare occasions the bitter cold refused to release its grip on the land.

The people who populated this old world endured a very difficult life. With most of the food sources buried under a thick cover of snow and the drinkable water frozen for much of the year, survival had been a constant battle. All of the people, the young and old alike, had to be resourceful, cunning and hard working just to keep fed. Nothing at this time had been easy, nothing ever taken for granted.

But the people survived.

This was how it was, until the day an unknown man came to live among the people. No one in the village seemed to know exactly when or how he arrived, but all the same, one day he was there.

This man's name was Noel Kringle.

It was not long after Noel joined the people that things started to change. The sun began to show itself in the sky more often. The snow and ice that had covered the land for so long began to melt away. Trees and grasslands sprang up everywhere. Flowers bloomed and rivers ran across green fields. Animals, finally released from their winter dungeon, prospered and multiplied. They filled themselves with the lush grass and leaves that were now, almost magically, everywhere.

And as the ground that had been frozen for as long as the people could remember began to soften, they found a deep and healthy earth that was easily tilled. Crops were planted and grew quickly. Very soon, what was once only icy tundra was now covered with vegetable fields and fruit groves. Food became plentiful and life became much easier for the hard working people.

Most of the villagers looked at Noel as being the cause of this miraculous change. Some believed that with his arrival, a curse that had pledged the lands was finally lifted. The people showered him with praise and gifts and even begged him to become their King.

But Noel would have none of it.

"I am but a simple man," he told them. "I till the earth and tend the crops just the same as all of you. I do not deserve any more praise then the next man. Living among such fine people is thanks enough for any good fortune I may have brought."

Then Noel would nod casually at the village folks and slowly walk away, kicking at pebbles along his path. He would look up at the beautiful blue sky and his lips, hidden beneath a thick, brown beard, would curl into a satisfied smile.

Many of the people were convinced by the sincerity of Noel's words. He was just a man, like any of them; worthy of no more than one or less than another.

But some others were not so convinced. They believed this man was hiding a secret. They whispered among themselves about what it could be. None of them, however, seemed to have any notions. They just knew there was something different about Noel Kringle.

And they were right.

Time passed, as it always does. The people of the village and its surrounding lands began to forget the cruel winters that were left behind with the arrival of Noel.

Winter still came of course. As did spring and summer and fall. But now a person could almost set the time by its arrival. Just as the last colorful autumn leaves fell from the trees, the blue sky would fill in with huge, fluffy white clouds. Then, within two or three days, the ground would be covered by a thick layer of fresh snow. But this wintery blanket stayed only long enough to rejuvenate the hungry earth. Exactly two weeks before the first day of spring, when farmers were growing excited to begin seeding their fields, the sun would show itself again and the snow would disappear as quickly as it had arrived. The people would

10

again find the soil lush, rich and rested; ready to offer its nourishment to produce fine, new crops.

Noel, staying true to his word, would be in the fields, tilling and seeding along with all of the other farmers. In fact, some would say he even worked harder than many. When his fields were prepped and seeded, a task he often completed before most of the others, Noel would never hesitate to offer a helping hand to anyone in need; always with a smile and jovial banter.

One warm and sunny day, as Noel walked slowly through the village square, greeting his many new friends with a hearty hand shake or clap on the back, he espied a beautiful young maiden that he had not happened upon before. She was sitting on a small stool, gazing into a field of cherry trees that were just coming to blossom. A painting easel stood in front of her.

Without conscious intent, Noel found himself heading in her direction. Walking up behind her, he saw she was painting a picture of the landscape that lay before them. She was a wonderful artist. The picture seemed to come alive on her canvas. He could have sworn he saw the tiny movement of the tree leaves as if stirred by an imaginary afternoon breeze.

"You are a very good artist," he commented to her.

"Well, thank you kind sir," she answered, turning to look up at him. "I love to paint pretty things."

Noel was left momentarily speechless. Never before had he been so affected by a simple smile. Her cheeks were the color of alabaster kissed by the palest pink rose. Her long luxurious lashes teased him with each bashful flutter. And he found himself sinking into the allure of her deep blue eyes.

"If that is what you like, may I suggest you gaze into a mirror and paint the beauty of your own reflection." Noel was a little shocked at the uncharacteristic brashness of his words, yet he could not stop himself. "Because never before have I witnessed such perfect loveliness."

"My my, are you always this flirtatious with girls who you have just met?" While her demeanor was slightly scolding, her smile belied her question.

"No, I'm sorry miss. I am unable to explain what has come over me." Now it was Noel's turn to smile coyishly. "And, I must admit, I also find myself unable to take back any of what I have said. You are beautiful and I would be honored to get to know you better." He took a small step back and bowed in an exaggerated genteel manner. "Let me introduce myself; Noel Kringle at you service."

"Oh, I already know who you are." The maiden said as she stood up. "You have quite a reputation in this hamlet. I can say the most of what I have heard has been good.....though...." Her smile widened as she returned his bow with her own coquettish curtsey. "No one mentioned your brazen way with the ladies." She held out her hand for Noel to take into his. "My name is Nature. And I predict, Noel Kringle, that you and I are going to become very good friends."

And so they did.

From that day forward the two were almost inseparable. They had many things in common and found a great ease in each other's company. Soon friendship turned to love. And love, as so often happens when it is true and pure, turned to marriage.

They had a very large wedding. All of the people in the village were invited to the celebration. Even some town folk from other villages came for the day of festivities. It was a glorious event indeed.

Late on in the evening, when they were finally alone, Nature looked lovingly into her new husband's eyes.

"Now that we are husband and wife," Nature said. "We should not have any secrets between us."

Noel touched Nature's golden hair. "Of course. No secrets. Ever."

"Then please tell me my love, where do you come from?"

Noel smiled. "You ask me and I shall tell you the truth. I come from a valley that lies behind the Great Mountains."

Nature's blue eyes widened with surprise. "The Great Mountains? But none other than a bird or billy goat has ever crossed the mountains. They are too high and too sharp. It cannot be done."

Noel agreed. "For a mere man it would be impossible. But what I haven't told you, my dear, is that the valley I come from is the land of Wizards."

"Wizards," Nature echoed. "You, therefore, are a wizard yourself." Her tone was that of a statement, not a question and, though her eyes did remain surprised, her expression was one of calm understanding.

"Are you not surprised?" Noel asked, confused by her calm face.

Nature smiled at him. "My mind is bewildered, but my heart remains at peace for I knew there was a special magic about you. I have felt it since the day we happened to meet in front of that field of cherry trees."

"Well," Noel continued, returning her smile. "Prepare your mind for further bewilderment. I was the King of these wizards," he told her calmly. "I ruled over the land, just as did my father before me."

"But why would a King leave his subjects?" Nature asked. "Why did you venture over high mountains to a new land when you had people who looked to you as their ruler?"

"Because I failed them," Noel said sadly. "I allowed a poison to leech into the valley and infect my subjects with a disease that ultimately destroyed them."

"Oh my," Nature gasped. "What was this terrible disease?"

"It goes by many names, but you would know it as greed or selfishness." Noel looked into her eyes. As he continued to speak, Nature could see a look of deep sadness taking over her husband's face. "It is a powerful sickness," he said. "That attacks one's mind and heart. It turned good people bad. Everyone began to yearn for more than could ever be possessed. Too soon all the power, wealth and beauty in our world was not enough. Each wizard wanted more and more. One would destroy what another had, because it was more than he possessed, then, ultimately, what the first had would be destroyed by yet another for the same reason. Around and around it went and eventually led to a War of the Wizards that lasted for many years. And, as war always does, it destroyed everything that everyone had, and all those who had it. In its wake, all that remained of this beautiful land, and these powerful wizards, was ashes."

Nature felt overwhelmed by what she was hearing. Before this day she had only heard whispered tales regarding wizards. Now she was wed to the King of a race of wizards that had, by all accounts, allowed greed to destroy them. "How did you escape," she asked.

"To be a good ruler, one must possess both sides of emotion. The bad side, so decisions can be made that are for the betterment of the people, but often carry with them very unpleasant consequences. And also the good, compassionate side. Kindness and generosity. Love. When I realized I had lost my people to the evils of greed, I was able to hold on to the good that was inside me. I opened myself up and allowed only this goodness and love to flow through me. It pushed the evil out and, though I was too late to help my people, I was able to escape my dying land. And I brought with me all the goodness of a wondrous and magical people. The beauty and hope of a land that, because of my failure as ruler, had been destroyed by a disease of the heart."

Nature's eyes showed some surprise, but also a sudden understanding. "You used that power," she breathed softly. "To save our land. You made the weather change."

Noel's mouth curled into a smile beneath his beard. "I had found a new people," he said to his bride. "A people whom had known nothing but hardship and pain. They were living in a land that did not love them. And yet they still possessed a kindness and selflessness like none I had ever encountered before. Though I did not want to rule over them as I had the wizards, I felt in my heart that they deserved better. So I simply talk to the skies and the ground and the air, and convinced all of these powers of nature to return the good people's love."

"You make it sound like such a tiny thing," Nature said. "And yet it is larger than the oceans of the world. You saved us from misery."

Noel shook his head. "You and your people did not need saving. I have just made things a little easier."

Nature hugged Noel tightly. "You are a great man," she whispered in his ear, his long hair tickling at her nose.

"I wish only to be treated as a regular man," he said and kissed his new wife. "No more, no less."

Klaas and Jacques

As the years went by, the village, which was now a pleasant and lovely place to live, grew and grew. If you are able, try to imagine a single cherry lying on a table. Now imagine that cherry is an entire pie. And now imagine, if you can, that the table is filled with these pies. That is how much the village grew in size in only a few years. Life that is good will always multiply and expand.

Noel and Nature's love for each other also grew. And just like life, love will expand and multiply. It was not long before their family of two became four.

One short year after their marriage, Nature, with Noel by her side, gave birth to twin sons. It was a joyous time for the entire village as Noel held each baby up to the sky and christened them Klaas and Jacques Kringle.

As young children, the two boys looked exactly alike. It was even difficult for Nature to tell them apart. They would often try to fool her into thinking one was the other. And sometimes they would succeed.

But they could never fool Noel. With only a quick glance at the boys, he would immediately know which of his sons was Klaas and which was Jacques.

This fact, needless to say, frustrated the twins to no end.

As the boys grew, however, their similarities began to melt away. At first, it was their personalities that began to differ. Klaas was always filled with laughter and happiness. He made friends easily, spending much of his spare time inventing new toys and games for them to play. His imagination was broad. One only needed to hand him a simple wooden board and watch with wonder as he created an amazing toy or piece of furniture. Even at a very young age his woodworking skills were unmatched by any other craftsman in the village.

And, like his father, Klaas was very hard working. He dealt with all of his chores quickly and without complaint. Often, he would even help his brother complete his chores as well. It was seldom you would find Klaas in anything other than a fine and happy mood.

Jacques, on the other hand, was a quiet and somber young man. His nature was shy and he spent much of his spare time alone in his room. His creativity could be matched to that of Klaas, but in quite a different way. Jacques was an ingenious inventor of mechanical things. Most of his creations were items that served to make his life easier. He hated chores, and complained about them often. He was not as strong as his brother, and found working on the farm and in the fields very difficult. His muscles ached, his back ached, and his mind ached for things other than the tediousness of farm work. So, after the work was done, he would go to his room and invent things to make the laborious chores quicker and easier. He would stay up late into the night, tinkering and creating. Automatic cornhuskers, self driving tillers, fruit extractors (quite an ingenious device that would gently shake a tree just hard enough to cause all of its fruit to drop on to the ground, thus eliminating the need to pick the tree clean). He even invented a candle that would not burn down for thirty days, so he could work long into the evening without having to change the candle stick but once a month.

Because Jacques was able to make so many things to ease his life, one would have thought him to be a happy boy. And yet, despite all of these wonderful inventions, he remained unhappy. He was in an almost constant state of annoyance. People annoyed him with their simple minded willingness to do more than they had to. His parents annoyed him with their unrelenting love and devotion to each other. But most of all, his brother annoyed him. Oh, how Klaas annoyed and angered him!

When they were young children, Klaas and Jacques were good friends, always playing and joking and having fun together. Klaas would always try to help his awkward brother fit in better with friends, and always included him in activities and games. But as they grew, Klaas began to get bigger. He got taller by the day. His muscles grew strong and his back broadened. His beard grew long and his hair was thick.

Jacques, however, did not get strong. His height increased the same as his brother, but his muscles did not grow. No matter how much he would eat, Jacques remained skinny and weak. His arms and legs were long and thin. His hair was lifeless, and his skin was pale. So pale in fact, some of the local village boys would tease him with a rhyme,

> 'Jacques is so pale
> That in the winter he is lost,
> Because not one can see him
> Through the snow and the frost.'

Klaas would, of course, scold them for being cruel to his brother, but this made Jacques even more embarrassed.

Klaas! Always coming to the defense of your poor 'little twin', Jacques would silently curse his brother. *Yet, I am the first born, therefore the eldest. I should be the one doing the protecting. But no! You just love to show off the fact that no one will treat you unkindly because you possess more strength than I do. It is so unfair!*

So Jacques had stopped playing with his brother and the other villagers. But for years he remained jealous of Klaas' popularity. Not that he was interested in having his own friends- as was said earlier, people annoyed him and he was happier by himself. No, he was jealous of Klaas because he did not want his brother to have anything that he, himself, could not have. In Jacques' mind, this also seemed grossly unfair. *Klaas builds some silly toy or chair, and everyone in the village raves on and on about how talented and special he is. I create an amazing machine and yet continue to be ignored by the villagers. How lopsided and strange is this?*

Then, one cool, spring afternoon, Jacques happened to see his brother walking through the village. Klaas was wearing a long red coat and his beard was blowing this way and that in the light wind that whistled across the square. Children were running after him, shouting and cheering and pulling at his coat tails. Klaas, who was now close to adulthood, scrubbed their heads with his large hand, tussling their hair. Then he stopped and began rummaging through a leather sack that had been slung over his shoulder. To the children's delight, he pulled out one toy after another, handing them out to his excited flock.

Jacques' brow tightened with confusion and anger at this sight. His brother was just giving the toys away. Useless and silly things, yes, but why would he give them away and receive nothing in return?

At first it had made no sense to Jacques. No sense at all. But later that evening, as he sat tinkering in his room, Jacques suddenly had a thought.

It had seemed that Klaas gave his toys away and received nothing in return. But, in truth, did he receive something? Short of Noel and Nature, who also had the strange habit of giving things away with no payment in return, Klaas was the most popular person in the village. Could this fact be because he gave things away? Was his payment the friendship and immense popularity he received as a result?

Jacques had never shared any of his inventions with the villagers. He had always built them for himself, and kept them for himself alone.

Well, that will change, Jacques decided right then. *I can give things away too. Not for free certainly, but for the minimal cost of favors and food.*

He imagined never having to do chores again. This thought brought a crooked, unpracticed smile to Jacques' face.

And if the villagers thought that Klaas' silly trinkets and toys were special, wait until they saw what Jacques had to offer. Inventions and machines like nothing they had ever seen.

It made perfect sense in Jacques' mind. He would become more popular and important than anyone else in the village. The villagers would surely even make him their King.

And then, once they made him King, Jacques would exile his brother to the farthest reaches of the land. Maybe he would exile his parents too. And half the villagers for that matter.

With these thoughts swimming happily through his mind, Jacques continued with his work. The twisted, strange little smile lingered on his face for quite some time.

Noel's Visit

Time marched forward like an unrelenting soldier. The village and its population continued to thrive at an unprecedented rate. There were so many people, in fact, that they had no choice but to start spilling into the outlying areas of the land. New villages and towns sprang up everywhere. Life for all was good.

Klaas and Jacques became men. Jacques' plan of distributing his inventions to the people quickly became a reality. In fact, his machines became so popular that he was forced to open a factory to keep up with demand. And, because he did not want any of the regular villagers inside his factory, Jacques employed a small forest dwelling people, called elves, to work for him.

It did not take long for Jacques to realize that these elves, though less than half the size of regular humans, were an extremely skilled and hard working people. Soon, with the elves handling almost all aspects of production, Jacques was able to spend most of his time locked away in his shop at the back of the factory. This made him very happy because he found that even the work done in his own factory was mindless labor, best left to a lesser race. Jacques' mind was then free to create more amazing machines.

Klaas also built a small factory on the northern side of the village (opposite of his brother's, which was on the southern border) where he could construct toys and small furniture. Although Klaas did not require anyone to help him, it was seldom he was alone in his factory. His village friends stopped by regularly to chat and joke with him over a hot cocoa or cool drink. In fact, around the pot belly stove in the center of the factory's main room had become a popular place for the village folk to gather and discuss a day's events or share any tidbits of interesting news. It was a warm and happy place where anyone was welcome at anytime.

But of course Jacques had never set foot inside Klaas' toy factory.

One morning, just as the sun was peeking its glowing face over the Great Mountains, Klaas arrived at his factory to begin work. When he walked inside he was surprised to see his father sitting on a stool beside the pot belly stove. In his lap he held a piece of oddly colored wood.

Klaas noticed immediately that Noel did not look good. Under his white beard, his face looked pale and drawn in and his eyes, which usually sparkled with life, appeared tired and distant. He was slumped on the stool as though exhausted. Klaas had never known his father to look so old and he instantly became worried.

"Father," he said. "What a surprise to see you about so early. Are you here for a cup of my famous hot cocoa? I can whip up a pot right away. I've heard it said that there is none more tasty in all of the village."

Noel shifted uncomfortably on the stool and clutched the wooden board closer to himself, as though protecting it. "No, no. Don't trouble yourself son. I am only here for a moment. I need to get back to the farm and tend to the fields. Harvest time is just around the corner."

"Perhaps I should join you," Klaas suggested, trying his hardest to hide the concern in his voice. "I could use a day away from the shop."

"Hogwash," Noel grunted. "Your mother and I manage just fine. You need to build these toys and what nots for the children. Keeping the little ones happy is a far more important task than pulling a few pesky weeds from the ground."

Klaas sat down beside Noel. "What brings you here at this early hour, Father?" He glanced down at the board that Noel held but had still not mentioned. "Is there something I can do for you?"

Now Noel looked up at his son with a grave expression clouding his face. "I need to ask you for a favor, my son."

The Gift

A short time later, Noel left the toy factory. He was no longer in possession of the wooden board, as he had left it in the care of Klaas.

Despite the warm sun that now sat high in the blue, morning sky, Noel felt chilled and pulled his robes tightly around himself. He moved through the village very slowly, each step taken with precision and care. His bones creaked and ached with every movement. His body had been getting weaker and weaker in the past weeks, and Noel was fearful that soon he would be unable to walk without a stick.

Breath labored from his lungs as he climbed a slight hill. The Kringle farm was less than a half mile from Klaas' factory, but even short journeys were becoming difficult for Noel. He had to stop once and lean against a fence post so his galloping heart could calm inside his chest. Though he still felt chilled, he removed a cloth from his pocket and used it to dab perspiration from his brow. He gazed back towards Klaas' small factory with sad, tired eyes; then continued on his march towards home.

Klaas had indeed been correct when he observed that his father did not look well. If he however, had known the truth about Noel's deteriorating health, he would have surely forced his assistance upon the old man.

For Noel was dying. Although, by this point, he had been aware of his condition for quite some time, he had told no one, not even his loving Nature. This was his secret to bear alone; at least for now. There were a great many things that needed to be put in place before he would divulge his undeniable fate to anyone. And when this great work was done, he would finally be able to share the truth of his life with his family. At long last there would be no more secrets.

Noel looked up at the shimmering sky and, for just a moment, a small smile crept across his face.

Soon, he thought, *everything will at last be put right.*

Several weeks passed. Harvesting was coming to an end. Tree leaves were beginning to turn the colors of autumn and, though the sky was still clear and bright, a slight chill in the air nipped at noses and ears and finger tips. Wood was chopped and snow shovels were pulled out of sheds in preparation for the winter that was waiting to pounce like a hungry lion.

The sun was just setting in the early evening as Nature sat at the Kringle's kitchen table sipping a cup of hot cocoa. Her blue eyes, which were still as bright as the day she met Noel, watched the front door with anticipation.

 Then, just as she was lifting the cup of cocoa to her lips, the door burst open, startling her. Her hand jerked and the chocolaty drink spilled on to the crisp, white table spread.

Jacques now stood in the door way, looking down at his mother with an ever present annoyance showing in his stare. "Well?" he demanded, stepping into the tiny room and slamming the door closed. "What is so important that I had to leave my busy factory and journey over here to this dust bowl?"

"Good evening to you as well, my son," Nature replied as she dabbed at the stained table spread with a damp cloth.

"Yes, yes," Jacques groaned. "Good evening, good evening. I am a busy man mother. What is it you require?"

"We asked you many days ago to visit us tonight, and yet you still arrive late. I love you, my son, but sometimes you can frustrate me so."

"As I already told you," Jacques said. "I am a busy man."

"Klaas arrived an hour ago," Nature told him. "He is already in the back parlor with your father."

"Klaas builds toys," Jacques quipped with distain ringing in his tone. "I would wager he was not dragged away from anything too important."

"Let us waste no more time," Nature said. "We must join your father and brother. There are many things to be discussed."

Things to discuss? These words confused Jacques as he followed his mother into the back parlor. He could not bring to mind the last time he and his family had exchanged more than five words, and yet now there were *things to discuss?* Very odd.

But when they entered the parlor and Jacques saw his father's frail appearance, he understood. The old man was laying on the overstuffed day bed with a thick quilt pulled up to his shoulders. On his chest sat a brightly colored box, adorned with ribbons and bows of such an exquisite fabric as had never been seen before. The box rose and fell with every raspy breath that clawed its way from Noel's lungs. Klaas was sitting at his side and Jacques could easily read the truth in the dismal expression that covered his brother's face like a mask of despair. Jacques understood immediately that Noel was very sick.

No. Not just sick. Their father was standing at the brink of death on legs that were about to fail him. Soon Noel Kringle would be taking his leave of them.

Although at that moment Jacques did feel emotion stirring within him, even he was not exactly sure what emotion it was.

"Father," he said, moving farther into the room. Nature sat herself down in a chair behind him, but Jacques did not sit himself. Instead he stood over Noel and Klaas, gazing down at them with a blankness in his expression that neither his father nor brother could read. "I have arrived as requested."

"Good good," the old man grunted, shifting uncomfortably on his bed. The box that rested on his chest continued to bob up and down with his words. "Thank you for coming Jacques."

"Mother has told me there are things to be discussed," Jacques said. "And I am assuming these discussions will involve your impeding death."

Nature's breath caught in her throat. "Jacques!" she exclaimed, but Noel held up his hand, silencing her before she could scold her son further.

"No, no," he said to his wife. "One should not be troubled for speaking the truth. Our son is honest and direct, if not always tactful."

Nature and Klaas both glared angrily at Jacques, but he, quite naturally, ignored their stares. "What have you to say father," he said. "We are all here, so speak your mind."

"Yes," Noel agreed, nodding his head. "There are many things about myself that I have only divulged to your mother. I have my own reasons for this, and I do not apologize for the decisions that I have made. But now, as I am coming to my end, I shall start at the beginning."

Noel talked for some time, pausing only occasionally to sip water from a glass that sat nearby. His voice was grave and low. His sons, at times, had to lean in closer in order to hear the words that he spoke.

Noel told them everything. Where he came from. How he happened to arrive in the village. And most importantly, what he was.

As he relayed his story, Klaas listened intently and his face remained thoughtful and calm. But one could easily see that Jacques' expression was becoming angrier and angrier with each word that left the old man's lips.

Nearing the end of his story, Noel looked at his son and asked "Jacques, what troubles you?"

"I do not understand," Jacques responded. "Why you would not tell us earlier that you are a wizard? With the power that you possess, we could have ruled this land together."

Noel shook his head slowly. "I did not come here to rule. I came here to live. Just to live, my son. A simple life."

"A simple life?" Jacques echoed. "A simple life you say? And yet you choose to use your power to manipulate the weather. How is that living a simple life?"

"I did what I felt was right to help these people."

"But what about helping us," Jacques pushed on, motioning towards his brother. "If we are your sons, why did we not inherit your wizard magic at birth? Why are we just normal men?"

"You, my sons, are far from normal men. You are both extraordinary men."

"But we possess no powers of magic?" Jacques argued.

"Because I would not allow it!" Noel shouted, suddenly angered. Then he lost his breath and began to cough and wheeze uncontrollably.

Nature rushed to her husband's side and held his head in her arms, comforting him.

Klaas stood up and confronted his brother with rarely revealed anger. "Why must you upset him? He is a sick man and needs our support!"

"I meant nothing by it," Jacques said all too calmly, although his face did show mild surprise by his father's sudden outburst. "But, do you not feel as I?"

"No," Klaas said firmly. "I am content as I am. I do not need magical spells and wizardry to be a happy man."

"Let us cease our bickering," Nature said. Noel's coughing spell was passing and he straightened himself in the bed. The colorful box had slipped off his chest and lay atop the quilt. He picked it up and clutched it firmly in his thin hands. "I understand," Nature continued. "That all of this is quite surprising to you both, but your father has more to say. We must let him speak."

"Very well," Jacques grunted and sat down heavily on a chair. "Continue with your tale."

Klaas also reseated himself, but said nothing further.

"Thank you my sons," Noel said, his fit now fully past. "I apologize for losing control of my faculties, but you must hear my words and understand; the magic that dwelled within me was not clean. When I left my land, I had hoped the evil that destroyed my people had died with them. I tried to take with me only the good magic of the wizards. But just as day must have night, to possess good magic, you must also possess the bad. The poison had indeed crept inside my body, yet for a long time I did not know it. So once every year, on the first day of winter, I would expel my powers to help bring the Seasons to this land and a better life to its people. It was at this time that I would be momentarily weakened, allowing the poisonous magic to spread through me like a virus. As the village grew larger and larger, I was forced to use more magic each year. And each year the poison grew stronger. By the time I recognized the danger, it was too late. I was doomed to the same fate as the wizards I had ruled. But this I accepted without pause. I failed the wizards as their King, therefore I deserve a punishment no less than what they received."

"Noel, no," Nature began, tears welling in her eyes, but once again she was silenced by her husband.

"It is what it is, my love," he said to her. "You must learn to accept the inevitable truth as I have." He touched her hand gently. "But the people of this village, and all of this beautiful land, do not deserve this fate. If I allowed myself to pass on with the magic still within my body, it would have perished with me. This land that I have grown to love with all my heart would surely have been plunged back into the never ending winter that was its curse. All I have worked so hard to achieve would be lost." A tiny smile crept across Noel's face. "So, with some help, I have been able to banish the magic from my body. It no longer lives within me and, therefore, can no longer die with me."

"But if it is not in you," Klaas asked, "Then where did you banish it to?"

Noel touched the box that was resting on his chest. "This exact wooden box that you constructed for me some weeks ago."

"But that is just an ordinary box," Klaas said. "No more special than anything I make."

Noel held up his hand. "Now, now, my son. Everything you make is special in its own way." He ignored a small, yet obvious sarcastic groan from Jacques and continued, "But it is not the construction that makes this box strong enough to hold the power of the wizards. It is the wood. I brought it with me from the valley beyond the Great Mountains. This box is equally as magic as the magic it contains." Noel smiled again, "And now it is beautiful as well. Thanks be to one of your Mother's perfectly painted cloth papers that she has so lovingly wrapped it in."

Nature returned his smile. "Thank you, my love."

"A Gift in no truer sense of the word," the old man continued. "Meant for all the men, woman and children of this land. The never ending winter that plagued these people can now forever be controlled." He touched the Gift gently with his thin, trembling fingers. "Once a year, as fall is coming to an end and winter's angry face is just beginning to show its ugliness, your mother, my beautiful Nature, will open the Gift and the power of the seasons will be renewed and keep winter only as lengthy as it should be." Noel looked from Jacques to Klaas, then back to Jacques again. "Hear me, my family," he said, staring into his son's eyes. "For this is very important. The Gift is to be opened only once a year, and only by Nature. Once a year, for a very precise amount of time, the length of which I have discussed with your mother. Then the box is to be closed up and not, under any circumstances, is it to be opened again until the same time the following year. And again I stress, only by Nature."

"Mother?" Jacques queried. "Why mother?" His face was expressionless, but his eyes blazed with anger. "Why not me? Am I not skilled enough to open a simple box once a year?"

Noel, again ignoring his son's belittling tone, answered; "The magic I have put inside the Gift is very sensitive to emotion. It will feed off of the inner moods and desires of the one who opens it. Klaas is passionate and kind, always generous, giving to all those around him. I am fearful the box would take advantage of his kind nature and, though I know he would try to use the magic only for good, the evil is powerful and would twist everything to serve its purpose. And Jacques, you are also passionate, but yours is self focused. You are ambitious and always motivated to advance your own position. The evil of the box would use you to serve its purpose even more easily, I fear, than your brother. Your mother, however, is compassionate and generous, but also strong willed and focused. She will not be manipulated by people or the magic of the box. She understands, better than anyone I have come across, the balance of nature and all the life forms that make it special. My Nature will always remember why the Gift is being opened, and never allow emotion to affect her judgment. Much of the power I have put inside the Gift is good and will help our people and the land that supports them. But we must not forget that evil also dwells inside the box, for there is never good without bad. Remember that evil is always eager to destroy all in its path, just as it did to the Wizards of the Valley so long ago."

When Noel finished, Jacques immediately began to shake his head, as though he could not believe what he was hearing. "So what, then, is our part?" He questioned, but did not wait for a response. "For we have inherited no magic from you when we were born, we inherit no magic from you now as you stand at the brink, and we are, as you have explained quite elegantly, too weak minded to even open a box once a year. So then, I ask again, what is our part?"

"You and your brother are the protectors of the Gift. It can never be allowed to fall into another's hands. It must stay always hidden and secret. The opening of the box by anyone other Nature would spell almost certain doom for all of the people. So you must always protect it and your mother."

"What would happen," Klaas pondered, "If someone other than mother opened the box?"

"I truly do not know," Noel answered, his head shaking back and forth with regret. "But this magic destroyed a civilization of powerful wizards, so I dare not consider what it could do to the gentle people of this land."

"But what, then, will happen when we grow old," Klaas now asked. "What shall become of the box after we are gone?"

"That, my family," Noel said. "Cannot happen. You must all exist as long as the box does. Your fates are tied to the Gift and you will remain until it no longer does."

Jacques stood up suddenly. "What?" He exclaimed. "What are you saying? Eternal life?"

"I am saying exactly what I am saying," Noel said calmly. "As long as the Gift exists, then so does my family. If it remains for an eternity, then so shall you."

"So we are to exist forever," Jacques repeated. "Doing what? Protecting a box? You give us no magic and now tell us that we are to live forever as the guardians of a box that is to be opened but once a year by mother? And what of our lives? What are we to do with an eternity?"

"Continue to do as you are doing now," Noel replied. "Be friends to the people. Grow with them and support them. Teach them about your machines and help them to be self sufficient. And Klaas, you guide the children. Show them how to appreciate what they have and the importance of growing into generous and independent adults. These tasks, in themselves, are worthy of two eternities."

Jacques' eyes were wide and angry. "You silly old man," he shouted. "How dare you presume to know me and what is good for me!"

Both Nature and Klaas stood up to confront Jacques, but Noel only looked at him with a face that was blank of emotion. "This is fine," he said to his wife and son, but his eyes never left Jacques'. "My son is welcome to express how he feels. Soon he will see the error in his words.....and in his heart. Fear not for Jacques, as he is a great man."

"You have robbed us of our birth right," Jacques said. "We should be powerful wizards as were you, destined to be Kings of the people. And yet now you ask us to be teachers? And friends? You silly, silly man."

"This is your destiny my son, as it is your mother's and your brother's. And my destiny is to pay a penance for my failures. I am able to do this freely and without fear, for I know that I am leaving all things in the hands of the finest and most noble family in the land. You are Kringle. That is your birth right."

"Jacques," Klaas said, stepping closer to his brother. "Father is right. We are a family and must stay loyal to one another. Do not be angry. We should embrace the gifts that father has bestowed upon us."

"Gifts?" Jacques echoed the word with distain in his tone. "Oh brother, how gullible you are. You accept all words spoken, regardless of their true meaning. Yet, what choice do I have but to accept this that has been forced upon me. I will, of course, do as you bid, my father." He bowed down to Noel in what could only have been a mocking gesture. "I will carry out the tasks you set before me." Then he straightened up again and pointed his boney finger at his father. "Hear me, though, as I speak only the truth. This is not my real destiny. You have trapped me into an eternal life that I do not care to live. But one day I will change all things. My true destiny still awaits and I will have it."

Then Jacques turned and left the room.

After he was gone, the three remaining Kringles had listened as the front door of the little house open and then close once more with a loud slam. They looked at each other quietly for a moment, all taking in the peaceful silence of the room.

When finally Noel did speak, it was with a quiet calm. "Well, that transpired just about exactly as I had anticipated."

"Sometimes that boy can be quite rude," Nature sighed.

But her husband disagreed. "Nonsense," he said. "He is just stubborn. He will come around in no time at all, I'm sure."

"Do you really believe that to be true," Klaas asked, sounding doubtful.

"Of course I do. He is a Kringle." Then Noel looked at his wife. "My love, would you fetch us a cool drink from the kitchen. My water glass has long been empty and all this talking has left me feeling positively parched."

"Certainly," Nature said. "Would you like something as well Klaas?"

"No thank you mother," he replied. Seating himself beside his father once more, Klaas ran his fingers through his long beard and sighed heavily.

"Do not fret, my son," said Nature. "Your father is correct. He will come around." Then she turned and exited the parlor.

Noel waited until he heard the clink and clunks of his wife tinkering in the kitchen, then he said to his son, "I am sorry to put all of this on you so suddenly my boy. It was unfair of me."

"I am your son and a proud Kringle," Klaas responded. "I accept all that comes my way. Unlike my brother, I believe my destiny to be whatever is best for this land and its people."

"You are a good boy," Noel said. "And it pains me to do this, but I am forced to put more on your shoulders, my son."

"Do not despair, father, for my shoulders are strong. Tell me what you require and it will be done."

Noel nodded. "Of course," he said, sounding very tired. "I chose not to discuss this in front of your mother, because she is very protective of both her boys, as am I. But this must be addressed. I fear that your brother may have inherited more from the Wizards of the Valley than I had foreseen. I feel a greed growing inside of him. I believe it to be the same greed that poisoned my people. I have tried to tell myself day after day that I am wrong. That he is simply ambitious and, while maybe more than a little bit selfish, the good inside of him will prevail. And yet, I cannot deny my fears. If he indeed possesses the poison of my people, he must never, under any circumstances, be allowed to open the Gift. Though I have already told you that if *anyone* opens the box other than your mother there would be dire consequences, I also believe if the poison that may affect Jacques is allowed to meet the evil that dwells in the box, the outcome could be disastrous beyond our comprehension."

"But why would he open the Gift?" Klaas asked. "He will heed your warnings."

"He is my son and I love him dearly, so I must believe that he will obey all that I have said. But a poisonous greed is a powerful thing. It can twist a man's mind and cause him to act unwisely, regardless of the consequences."

"What will you have me do, father?"

Noel considered this for a moment before saying, "Be his guardian. Teach him the error of his selfish ways."

Klaas sighed again. "That will be no small task. Jacques is.....stubborn."

"But you will prevail," Noel said. "You must." The old man reached out and laid a trembling hand on his son's shoulder. "For, though it wounds me deeply to tell you this, it is also for your own good; as his twin, Jacques' fate shall also be yours. Since the day of your birth, you have been bonded with your brother as one. His failures will be yours as well. And his punishments will be shared by you. I wish that it was not this way, my son, but I am powerless to change it. So you must succeed and show Jacques the error of his ways. I know there is good in him still and I pray you will find it."

"Fear not," Klaas said. "For I too know there is good in him. If I were to ever give up on my brother, then I would surely deserve to share his fate." Then Klaas leaned over and hugged Noel. "I shall miss you more than you can ever know, Father."

"And I you," Noel said as he embraced is son. "But always remember; though I will be gone from this land, and this body, if you are ever truly in need, I will be there for you. This, my son, is my solemn promise to you."

Claira

On a sunny autumn afternoon, two days after the family had met in the tiny back parlor of the Kringle house, Noel fell asleep and did not wake up. Though the news of his passing brought great sadness to all the people of the land, they did not mourn. Instead there was a wondrous celebration in the village to honor the life of this great man. All the people from all the villages joined together to remember the deeds of Noel Kringle. For many years after, this celebration of life was said to be the largest gathering in the history of the village.

As one year became two and two became many, the village folk continued to live on as always, despite the great loss of Noel. Jacques' factory rumbled on, producing machine after machine, and invention after invention. Distribution of his amazing creations was far and wide, reaching the limits of even the farthest towns. It would have been easy to say that Jacques' machines were known throughout the land. And yet, Jacques himself remained shadowed by the popularity of his brother. Though he did attempt to be kind to his fellow man, Jacques would always end up angered and annoyed by the mere presence of other people. His temper would flare up and, ultimately, he would say or do something rude. And when the people stormed away from Jacques, hurt and upset by his cruelty, he would shake his head in confusion. As far as he was concerned, not one of the villagers had any more sense than a hound dog; so that is how he treated them. When he reprimanded one, it was for the good of that person. In his mind, they should thank him for his wisdom, not run off in a silly snit.

Because of this coldness that dwelled within his heart, many children- who are always the most honest of people- began to call him 'Jack Frost'.

Klaas also continued to work in his factory, producing toys for the children or furniture for those in need. And because of his kindness and intelligence, it was not long after the passing of his father that the people began to look to Klaas for advice and assistance regarding the interests of the village. It was even quite often that the town meetings were held around the pot belly stove in his factory. Klaas would insist on making his famous hot cocoa for all who arrived. He would not, however, allow any of the villagers to call him the town 'Leader'. Using the words of his Father, he would say simply, "I am just a man. No more than one, no less than the other."

Nature remained on the Kringle farm and, although Klaas insisted on doing most of the field work, she still ran her home as she always had. Cooking and cleaning and baking and canning used up most of her time. But, with any spare time that she did have, Nature would spend it painting. With her skill and imaginative use of color, she was able to produce landscapes of such beauty that they rivaled those which the land itself had created. Like her sons, Nature was also becoming known far and wide for the realistic and colorful beauty of her art. There was at least one Nature painting hanging on the wall of almost every house in the village.

The Gift Noel had left in his wife's care also remained in the Kringle house, hidden away in a spot of Nature's choosing. Each year, on the first day of winter, and with Klaas standing protectively outside the house, she would retrieve the box from this hiding spot. Then she would carefully remove the cloth paper, uncovering the well-crafted wooden vessel beneath. And, just as her husband had instructed her, she would close her eyes, hold her breath, and then open the lid of the box.

Even through her closed eyelids, Nature could see the brightness of the brilliant light that exploded from the Gift. She would feel a heat on her face, calming and warm as though she were facing into the sun. This light would shine fiercely for some time, and then it would blink out, extinguished just as quickly as it had begun. Opening her eyes again, Nature could now look inside the box and see just its simple wooden interior. Nothing more.

She would then re-wrap the Gift lovingly and place it back where it belonged, hidden away until the following year.

Winter would still come, as it always did. But with the opening of the box, its life would be no longer than that of its sisters- spring, summer, and autumn. Spring would be set free upon the land, extinguishing winter just as the light of the Gift had been extinguished.

And that is how things went for many, many years.

Until one day, just as spring was shining down from the sky and melting away the last traces of snow from the ground, a lovely young maiden came to live among the people. She was a teacher of children and had been invited to join the village and help with the schooling of their ever growing population.

Her name was Claira and she was indeed more beautiful than any other maiden in the village. Her hair was as golden as the sun and the smile of her deep red lips would have surely stopped any suitor in his tracks. Yet, the beauty of her face was dimmed in comparison to the beauty of her heart. She was a kind and gentle woman who was friendly with everyone she met and relished in the teaching of children. There was never an unkind word that crossed her lips and she unwaveringly believed that all people, be them kings or peasants, were equal. She loved life and life, in turn, loved her.

One day, not long after she arrived in the village, Claira happened across the path of Jacques Kringle. She was walking towards the schoolhouse, her arms full of books, and Jacques was proceeding towards his factory in the opposite direction. As they passed, Claira smile at Jacques and bid him a fine morning. Jacques, of course, said nothing in return, but his eyes suddenly widened and he stopped dead in the middle of the walk way. He turned and watched as the maiden continued along the path away from him.

Never before had Jacques been taken by the beauty of a woman. Most he found to be as equally annoying as anybody else, and he had not the patience for them. But this maiden who had just passed by him, was so captivating that even Jacques' icy heart began to thaw. He felt a tingling warmth move through his body. Such a warmth, in fact, that the tips of his ears had surely become hot to the touch. The small twisted smile that always looked so awkward upon his face, now stretched from one of his ears to the other.

He remained riveted to this spot, watching as she drew farther and farther away, and continued to watch even after she had turned a corner, disappearing from sight. Then finally, several moments after she was gone, Jacques reluctantly turned himself around and in a love struck daze, continued his journey towards the factory.

From that time on, Jacques found it very difficult to concentrate on anything else beyond this young maiden. When he was working in his shop, her small round face and green eyes would continually cloud his thoughts, making it increasingly challenging to focus on the job at hand. He would glance at the time piece on his work bench, then almost immediately get lost in his thoughts and the next time he looked at the clock, he would be shocked to see that the better part of two hours had past, yet not a lick of work had he accomplished.

Jacques was able to learn from the elves that the young girl's name was Claira (though how a group of tiny factory workers were able to learn this remained a mystery to him). She had come to the village as the new school teacher. Jacques felt a mild disappointment after learning these two pieces of information. First, he thought that Claira was a very plain, normal sounding name. Something more regal, like Victoria or Elizabeth, would have been much better. And second, Jacques could not abide children. They were small and useless creatures that could not think nor care for themselves. They were generally dirty and at times even smelly. Attempting to teach them anything would most definitely be a laborious and tiring task. He wondered to himself why a woman as beautiful as Claira would choose such an unfulfilling way to pass the time.

But because of her beauty, Jacques was willing to over look these flaws. He began to make every effort to cross paths with her again. He learned (again from the elves) what time she would arrive at the schoolhouse and what time she generally left. Then he would make sure that he happened to be walking along the pathway at those same times so they could meet again. He also devised many different conversations that they could have together. He was quite sure that one who spends so much time around children must be starved for any interesting and intelligent topics of word transactions. Although Jacques did not have much practice, he was confident that he would be an excellent conversationalist if the person he was talking to was worthy of sharing his brilliance.

Then something very strange and unexpected began to happen. Each time Jacques passed by Claira on the walkway, she would smile and bid him a good day. Yet instead of returning her good will or beginning one of the conversations he had practiced over and over, Jacques' mind would go completely blank and he would stare at the ground. Without even slowing the stride of his walk, he would continue past her as though she were not there.

Though this bizarre reaction confused and frustrated Jacques, it did not seem to matter what he did or how hard he tried; each meeting ended with this same dismal result. He could not mumble so much as a sound to this woman of his dreams.

Things continued on this way for quite some time. Jacques was just facing the difficult conclusion that he should give up his pointless quest, when one sunny summer afternoon, something happened that changed his luck for the better. As always, he was walking up the pathway and had just spied Claira coming towards him with, as was usual, her arms full of books. As he drew nearer to her and his heart was beginning to beat harder inside his chest, which was also not unusual, a group of children sudden appeared behind Claira. Shouting and cheering and singing her name happily, they all rushed around the schoolteacher. Though she was startled only a little bit by the children, some of the books she carried slipped from her arms and landed on the dirt pathway.

Jacques immediately felt anger welling inside of him and all of his inhabitations melted away to wherever they had come from. He balled his hands into tight fist and rushed over to the little group.

"How dare you startle this young woman that way!" he shouted at the children. "Have you no manners or discipline? Are you all being reared by wildebeests?"

Claira's eyes widened with shock at this angry outburst, but the kids seemed quite unsurprised. "Sir," Claira began. "That is really not..."

But Jacques stopped her. "I will deal with this, my lady," he said to her quickly before shouting at the children again. "Be gone from here you insolent pack of nose miners! This lady shall not tolerate your bothersome presence any further!"

Though the children did begin to back away from Jacques, they were all snickering behind their hands.

"Be gone!" Jacque shouted again. "Or a firm clout you shall receive!"

"Good bye Missy Claira," the children chortled as one, and then turned and headed off. But as they ran away, they chanted, "Jack Frost, Jack Frost! His heart is frozen and his mind is lost!!"

"Brats," Jacques grumbled under his breath as he began to pick up Claira's fallen books. "Should be caged with the beasts."

When he straightened up again, there was an awkward smile pulling at his lips. With a slight bow in his gesture, he handed the books back to Claira. "Your books," he said softly.

Claira's eyes were still wide and the smile that appeared between her cheeks was as equally awkward as the one that painted Jacques' features. "Thank you, sir," she responded politely.

Jacques' hands were again balled into nervous fists at his sides and he stared intently at the ground, as though it were some special thing he had never seen before. "My name is Jacques," he said, almost too quietly to hear. "Jacques Kringle."

"Well thank you... Jack," Claira repeated.

Jacques' head immediately flew up and his eyes blazed. "Jacques," he corrected her, his tone sharp.

"Oh," Claira gasped. "I'm sorry. Jacques."

Jacques looked back down at the ground. "I did not mean to snap at you," he apologized. "But the children...sometimes they...taunt me."

"I heard," Claira agreed. "I do appreciate your gallantry and your kind assistance with my books, but I must say this; do you not think that children should be treated more as people than as mere annoyances?"

Jacques frowned. "If people are annoyances, then I treat them as such. It matters not whether they are children or the children's parents."

"I see," she said, shifting her books uncomfortably from one arm to the other. "Well Jacques, my name is Claira and it has been very interesting meeting you, but now I fear I must be on my way. These books are beginning to weigh quite heavy."

"Yes, yes," Jacques snipped. "So you should. Off with you now." Then he stepped past her and started down the pathway, this time back towards where he had come from.

"Jacques," Claira called to him.

Jacques stopped in his tracks and slowly turned around. He stared at her questioningly, but said nothing.

"Were you not going that way?" Claira asked, pointing down the path in the other direction.

Jacques was silent for just a moment before saying, "I am returning to my factory to retrieve a thing which I have forgotten, if you must know."

"I see," Claira said again.

Jacques began to turn, but then looked back at the young woman. "If, by chance, we were to meet on this path again, sometime in the future, would it be prudent for me to speak to you again...at that time...in the future?"

Claira smiled at Jacques. "Well, as it seems that we pass each other every day along this very path, I think that would be fine." Then with light humor, she added, "But only if you have something interesting to say."

Jacques' brow creased. "If it was not interesting," he stated. "Why would I waste my time or yours by saying it?" Then he turned quickly and was gone in the same direction he had come from.

Claira watched him for a moment, the little smile still gracing her pretty face. *What an odd man*, she thought to herself. She then turned as well and hurried down the path towards home, hoping to make it before her arms weakened enough that she dropped the books all over the ground for the second time.

The next morning, as Claira was on her way to the schoolhouse, she once again found Jacques standing in the exact same spot they had just left the previous afternoon. A tiny smile teased her lips as she approached this skinny man with pale, pale skin. She had to stop herself from giggling when she thought again of the song the children had sung to taunt him, 'Jack Frost, Jack Frost'.

Claira stopped in front of him and said, "Good morning, Jack.....Jacques" She corrected her error without him noticing.

Jacques looked up at the blue sky. "Yes, I suppose it is an adequate morning," he replied. "Though I do wish it were cooler."

"Well winter will be here soon enough I'm sure." Claira said. They both stood silently for a moment, each staring up at the sky.

"Jacques, can I ask you a question," Claira said, finally breaking the silence that was quickly becoming awkward.

"If you have a question to ask, then I see no reason you would not be able to ask it," Jacques replied. "Unless, in some peculiar way, you were suddenly struck dumb."

"Ok," Claira said hesitantly and with mild confusion in her tone. "I shall ask it. Yesterday, why did you chase off those children?"

"Why?" Jacques thought about this for a moment before answering. "Because they are pestilent little creatures who have no regard for the comfort and personal space of others."

"I see," Claira said. "So it did not occur to you, in any fashion, that they were just happy to see their teacher outside of the schoolhouse and were reacting in the joyous manner that is a child's tendency?"

Now it was Jacques' turn to look confused. "I do not understand your statement."

"It is quite simple, Jacques," Claira said. "And I am telling you this only in an attempt to help you grow and become a better person." Jacques brows shot up with surprise at this comment, but he remained silent, allowing her to continue. "Children are innocent and naïve to the ways of the adult world. They do not hide their feeling behind false modesty or in an attempt to protect their vanity. How they feel is expressed through actions.

Joy is expressed through excitement and happiness, loud calls, singing, jumping up and down. Anger is in turn shown by tears or tantrums. Yesterday, what you saw was joy and yet you reacted with anger."

Jacques smiled his small, twisted smile. "You, Claira, sound just like my brother."

"Klaas," Claira agreed. "Yes, your brother and I share several views when it comes to children."

The smile instantly vanished from Jacques' face. "You know my brother?"

"Yes. Everyone knows Klaas Kringle. Plus, he comes by the schoolhouse quite often with toys for the children. He is such a kind and giving man."

"So I've heard," Jacques quipped. He contemplated this for a moment before continuing. "And the new stove in the schoolhouse? Is it working well? Keeping things warm in the winter with minimal wood burn?"

"Yes, I do believe it works quite well. And I've heard," Claira added, "That it required the school master to forfeit five bushels of corn and ten baskets of berries. Quite a costly item, to be sure."

"Sometimes genius garners a high price from those who do not possess it."

"Yes indeed it does," Claira agreed. "As does friendship, for those who do not have the peace of mind to acquire it." Claire shifted her books from one arm to the other. "I should be getting to the school now. The morning hour is growing late."

"Yes, yes. It is time to begin the day."

Claira stepped past Jacques. "Goodbye, Jacques," she said.

"Claira?"

She turned and looked at Jacques again. "Yes?"

"Was this a good conversation," he asked. "Was it adequately interesting?"

"Yes," Claira said. "It was indeed interesting."

"Then we shall speak again," Jacques confirmed with renewed confidence, then was gone down the path.

Claire watched him, her head slowly shaking from side to side. "And I am sure that too, will be an interesting conversation," she said softly.

Claira and Jacques' conversations on the pathway to and from the schoolhouse continued for several more weeks. At times, the odd things that Jacques would say made Claira giggle. Other times, however, she found herself resisting the urge to reach out and slap him across the face. This reaction went strongly against her nature and left her feeling ashamed. Yet it was an impulse that was impossible to deny. Though she often felt sorry for this strange, skinny man, she could not help but wonder if he was capable of being much more dangerous than anyone would suspect. But then she would tell herself she was being irrational and silly. He was no more than an eccentric man with very self-focused views on life. He was harmless.

Then one morning, Jacques told her something that rekindled her fear of just how unpredictable he truly was.

"One day very soon," Jacques said, after they had exchanged their standard greeting pleasantries. "I will be King of this land and ruler of its people."

"Oh," Claira exclaimed. Of all the strange statements that had come from Jacques' mouth, this one surprised her more than any other. "I did not realize you descended from royalty."

"I come from the highest grade of royalty that has ever existed," Jacques announced. "To become King is my birth right and my destiny. Soon it will also be a reality."

Claire was flabbergasted. "I see," she whispered. "And the people you are to rule? Do they know of this?"

Jacques looked confused. "Know? What is it they are required to know?"

"Well, Jacques," Claire said slowly, as if talking to a young child. "Do they know that they are to soon be ruled over by you? Are they agreeable with this surprising development?"

Jacques smiled. "People are like sheep. They know not where to venture without first being shown. I am the sheep dog that will herd them. I shall guide them down the right path."

54

"Oh. And how is it you shall guide them?"

Jacques shook his head. "This," he said, suddenly sounding frustrated, "Is not the purpose of our conversation. All these questions you are asking shall be, if necessary, discussed at another time."

"Then what, Jacques, is the purpose of this conversation?"

"I wish you to be my Queen," Jacques said proudly.

Claira's eyes widened and one of the books that she was holding slipped out of her arms and fell onto the pathway. Jacques quickly picked it up and handed it back to the dumbfounded maiden.

"What say you," Jacques asked again after a few moments of silence. "Will you be Queen to my King?"

"Are…." Claira had to clear her throat as she was having a hard time finding her voice. "Are you asking me to marry you?"

Jacques groaned. "Unfortunately, the union between a man and a woman does require this symbolic and, in my opinion, pointless ritual called marriage. So, I suppose that, yes, I am asking you to marry me. What say you?"

"But Jacques," Claira said, "We have only known of one another for a few weeks. Through our occasionally conversations on this pathway, I have learned very little about you, while you in turn know even less about me…."

"That matters not," Jacques replied, but Claira held up her hand, stopping his words.

"Beyond that, Jacques," Claira continued, "Though it pains me to say this, we have nothing in common what so ever. We are two opposite sides of a single coin."

"And yet," Jacques added, "Joined together by the mere fact that it is indeed a single coin."

"I do not believe that you are understanding what it is I am trying to say."

"I understand everything," Jacques said, his tone becoming louder and more agitated. "I am brilliant and shall soon be the most powerful man in all this land. You are the most beautiful woman in all this land. What more do we need in common than that?"

"Do you not see, Jacques," Claira said. "That this is the exact reason we can never be together. You see me only as beautiful, nothing more. You care not about what my heart feels or what matters to me. I could never love a man who sees only my skin and not what thrives beneath it."

"Who is talking about love?" Jacques asked, his eyes now blazing with anger.

"I am," Claira shouted at him. "For I am in love with another."

Jacques expression did not change, as though he had not heard what she said.

"Did you not hear, Jacques?" Claira asked, but then continued without waiting for an answer. "I am in love with another man. And he loves me as well, but not because I am beautiful. He loves my heart. He loves the person that I am. We are to be married three days from now."

Now Jacques did hear and the sudden comprehension twisted his face with rage. "Why did you not tell me this before," he demanded, his voice fierce.

"Because I was afraid of hurting you," she replied. "But now I clearly see that you possess nothing that can be hurt. All that resides in you is your self-worth and a writhing desire for power."

"You know nothing," Jacques growled. "What I possess is beyond anything you could ever understand. I shall be King. I will be the most powerful King that this land has ever seen. And you shall regret the decision you have made." Then Jacques turned and stormed away from Claira.

"You may very well become King," Claira called after him. "But you will rule no one! These people will never follow you!"

Jacques threw his arms in the air as he walked, but said nothing further.

Claira watched him until he disappeared over the rise of a hill. After he was lost from her sight, she sat down on the concrete stoop that ran beside the pathway and began to cry. Her tears spilled down her cheeks and dropped onto the books she still held, darkening the covers to a deep crimson.

The Toy Factory

The same day that Jacques announced to Claira that he would King, Klaas was traveling to another village. His wagon, which was drawn by two strong reindeer, was loaded high with toys for the children and some fruits and vegetables for any who were less fortunate than himself. He was gone for the entire day, and did not return to his factory until the sun was low in the sky.

At that time, as Klaas approached, he saw that Claira was sitting on a stool by the front door of the factory. He smiled happily and with a little shake of the reins, the pair of reindeer leapt forward into a gallop.

Claira stood and smiled as Klaas stopped the wagon in front of the wooden building.

"Hello, my dearest Claira," Klaas exclaimed. "What a lovely surprise to see you here at this hour of the evening." He jumped down from the wagon and embraced the young maiden in his arms.

"Oh, how I've missed you, Klaas," Claira said, tears beginning to well up in her eyes. "Please, do not ever leave me again." She buried her face into the thickness of his shoulder and began to weep.

"My love," Klaas said with concern ringing clear in his tone. "I have only been gone but a single day. Our day of marriage is still two sun rises away. There is plenty of time to prepare."

"I know," she sobbed. "And I long for that moment when I can become your wife. It would be impossible for the joyous day to arrive too quickly."

"Then why do you cry, Claira?" Klaas asked. "What is upsetting you?"

"I am frightened," Claira told him. "I am so frightened."

"Frightened?" Klaas frowned as he led her into the factory. He set her in a chair by the pot belly stove, then knelt down and took her face in his hands. "What is it that frightens you? I tell you, there is nothing in this land that I would not protect you from."

"Your brother," she said.

"Jacques?" Klaas was surprised by this, and yet a smile came to his face. He chuckled softly in an attempt to lighten the mood.

But Claira would have none of it. Instead she became even more upset. "You laugh at your future wife?" She sobbed into her hands.

"No, no," Klaas replied quickly. "Never would I laugh at you." He lifted her face up and looked into her wet eyes. "You are to be my bride and I love you more than anything in this land," He said. "I only chuckled because I think everyone is a little afraid of my brother, in one way or another. But I assure you, he is harmless. What did he do that has upset you so?" Klaas brought a handkerchief from his pocket and handed it Claira.

Using it to dab away tears from her cheeks, Claira said, "It is not that he did anything. It is his words that have frighten me. He has told me the strangest things."

"That is generally his way," Klaas agreed. "What was it he said?"

"He told me that he would be King of this land. He said it was his destiny."

Klaas smiled again, although if Claira had looked into his eyes she may have noticed the touch of worry that now showed in them. "That is a tale I have heard many times myself. But I promise you, my love, it is meaningless. Soon he will find a new project to dwell on and he will forget these silly ideas."

"How can you be so sure," she asked him.

"Because he is my brother and I know him well," Klaas assured her. "He talks and talks, but deep down inside he is a good man, with a good heart. He is just very bad at showing it."

"He asked me to be his Queen."

"Oh," Klaas breathed. "That *is* surprising. I did not think Jacques agreed with the sanctity of marriage. Did you tell him you were betrothed to another?"

Claira nodded. "Of course. He became very upset and stormed away."

"Well, there you are," Klaas said calmly. "He stormed back to his factory, locked himself away in the back room, and is no doubt in the midst of creating some sort of new gadget. He has probably already forgotten about the whole incident." Klaas paused for a moment, and then asked, "Did you tell him it was I who had won your hand?"

"No," Claira confirmed. "I did not! You did not see him, Klaas. He was so angry. I am afraid of what he might do when he finds out."

"Oh, I have seen him angry many times," Klaas said and touched Claira's cheek gently. "Since my father left us long ago, I have watched Jacques very closely. In that time, I have come to believe that behind the anger and insolence, there is the heart of a good man. Jacques is stubborn and single minded, but I am confident he would not act out in such a way as to harm another person. He is my twin brother, and I have never sensed anything inside of him that need be feared by anyone."

"But what if you are wrong?" Claira asked doubtfully.

"Trust me my love," Klaas said and kissed her softly. "I am not wrong. I will go and talk with him tomorrow morning. I will tell him the truth; that you are the love of my life. Although at first he will surely be upset at not being the one to win your hand, I do believe that in time he will find happiness for us."

Claira sighed. "Ok. I hope it is as you say."

"He is my family," Klaas said, hugging his young bride tightly in his arms. "Family is love, and love, in the end, prevails."

The Machine Factory

The next morning, Klaas' wagon stopped in front of the machine factory. In truth, he had never actually been invited by Jacques; yet, Klaas had been inside the factory many times. He had learned a long time ago not to wait for an invitation to visit his brother. And though Jacques always acted irritated by these unannounced visits, Klaas was sure that somewhere, deep down, his twin was happy for the attention.

Klaas did not knock, but simply swung open the front door and walked inside. Despite the earliness of the hour, the elves where already behind their benches, hard at work. One of them, who Klaas understood to be the eldest of this group, stopped his work a rushed over to greet the new guest.

"Sir Kringle," the elf chortled happily. Though he had learned to speak the language of the village quite well, a thick elfish accent was still very evident. "What a great and unexpected happiness this is for me."

Remembering the old elf's name, Klaas replied, "Sming my good man, it is good to see you."

"Yes yes, good good Sir Kringle," the elf sang.

"Not Sir Kringle," Klaas said, as he had many times before. "Just Klaas. My name is Klaas. Sir Kringle, I believe, is my brother."

"Oh, yes, yes. Sorry, sorry. Kris. Just Kris."

Klaas chuckled and clapped Sming on the back. "Not Kris. Klaas."

Sming frowned. "Yes, Kris. What you say, it does not role off an elf's tongue too well. Kris, much better. Means good friend. Kris is fine name for you, yes?"

Klaas laughed again and then nodded. "Yes, ok. Kris is a fine name." He gazed around the factory and noticed at once that all the elves were staring at him with apprehension bordering on fear showing in their eyes. This seemed very odd, as they were usually happy when he paid visits to the factory.

"What is wrong here?" He asked Sming.

"Not a good day for visit," Sming told him. "Not good at all. Sir Kringle is grumpy. Very, very grumpy."

"When is Jacques not grumpy?" Klaas joked as he stepped past the elf to head towards a closed door at the back of the factory.

Sming followed after him frantically. "No, no! Worse today. Much worse! Mister Kris should come visit another day. That is better idea."

"Nonsense," Klaas said over his shoulder. "Seeing me will probably cheer the old man up."

"Don't think so," Sming pleaded. "Not today. Another day, yes. Today, no."

Klaas reached the door but did not open it. He turned to face Sming. "Trust me, my friend," he said. "Jacques is always happy to see me."

Then he opened the door and disappeared though it.

"Not today," Sming whispered again before reluctantly returning to his bench.

It was quite dimly lit inside the back shop. Only a single candle burned on top a large wooden bench, lighting up Jacques' face but little else. He was sitting behind this bench with his hands folded together in front of him. Usually, when Klaas entered Jacques work shop, he would find his brother bent over some machine with wrenches and tools scattered all around him. But today the bench top was clear and Klaas was surprised to see that Jacques was staring directly at him.

"Brother," Jacques said. "How pleasant it is that you have decided to pay my little factory a visit."

"Yes," Klaas agreed, feeling confused by his brother's pleasant demeanor. "It has been some time since we last met, so I thought it prudent."

"Well, it is fine to see you, Klaas," Jacques said. "Tell me, what news is there from the land outside my shop?"

"News?" Klaas repeated.

"Yes, news," Jacques said again. "Things of interest. Events. Parties..... weddings. That sort of thing. News...."

Realizing then his brother already knew the reason for his visit to the factory, Klaas smiled. "I do have some news for you, brother." He said. "Great, wonderous news. Two days from now, I am to be wed."

Jacques clapped his hands together suddenly, sending a crisp 'crack' sound echoing through the small space. "That is wonderful!" He exclaimed. "And what a coincidence. A female acquaintance of mine is also due to be wed in two days."

Klaas sighed. "Jacques, let us not continue this pointless bantering. It is quite obvious that you know I am the one who is betrothed to Claira. We are in love and shall marry day past tomorrow. I am sorry if this upsets you."

"Upset...... me?" Jacques said with a sarcastic smile turning up the corners of his mouth. "Why would I be upset? I have grown quite accustomed to this family....this Kringle family," he growled, "And their habit of stealing away everything I hold dear."

"You are also a Kringle, my brother," Klaas pointed out calmly, "Besides, nothing has been stolen from you. You must possess something as your own before it can be stolen."

"You have stolen everything from me!" Jacques shouted suddenly and jumped out of his chair so quickly that it fell back and clanked against the floor. "Father robbed me of the power that was my birth right! Mother stole away my Gift and hid it! Now you....my brother, have stolen the only person that has ever interested me!"

"Claira interested you," Klaas echoed, keeping his voice low and even. "And that, my dear brother, is why she would never have been any more than an acquaintance to you. She knows that she has no more worth in your eyes than one of your lifeless machines."

Jacques slammed his palms onto the desk top. "Do not presume to tell me how I feel! All you have done since the day Father died is tell me how I feel! Yet, the truth is you have no idea what thoughts dwell within my mind!"

"You must calm down, Jacques," Klaas said. "I have done nothing with the intent of hurting you. You are my brother and I love you. But I also love Claira and there is nothing I can do to change that. Please understand this."

Now Jacques did calm down. His shoulders slumped and his face went blank of any expression. "As Father was so fond of saying, there is no good without evil," he said, looking directly in Klaas' eyes. "Well I have come to learn that there is also no love without hate. And I hate you, brother. With all my heart I say this. We are no longer family. I banish the Kringle name from my mind forever."

"Jacques," Klaas pleaded. "Do not say these things, for I know they are not true. You have been hurt, but we can move past this, just as we always have. Do not give up on your family."

"Be gone from my factory," Jacques yelled. "Go and marry your....love. But do not return here ever. And do not look to find me again. I do not know you anymore."

"Jacques...." Klaas began, but could say no more.

"Be gone," Jacques repeated, and then turned his back to Klaas.

Klaas stood where he was for a moment, staring at his brother's back, trying desperately to figure out how things could have gone so wrong, so fast. But, realizing there was truly nothing more to say, finally he too turned, and left Jacques' workshop.

Once Klaas had left the machine factory, the elves all huddled together and stayed very quiet. They whispered among themselves, and looked to Sming for comfort, but he could find none to give. All they could do was watch the door at the back workshop and hope it did not open.

The Schoolhouse

Early in the morning, on the day before Klaas was to wed his love, Claira hurried down the pathway towards the schoolhouse. She knew in her mind that Jacques would not be in his usual spot, waiting for their daily conversation, but in her heart she was a little disappointed when she did not find him there. She stopped for a moment and looked at the concrete stoop where only two days earlier, she had sat crying. It seemed impossible that she could miss him, even after all the grief he had caused her. Yet she could not deny this truth; she had grown accustomed to, if not fond of, their daily chats.

Sighing, Claira continued on her way to the schoolhouse.

When she arrived, she climbed the three steps to the front door of the tiny building. Then, freeing one hand by balancing her books carefully on her hip, she let herself in.

Though it was still quite early in the morning, brilliant summer sunlight cascaded in through the schoolhouse's many windows, giving the interior a bright yellow glow. Claira made it almost half way into the room before she noticed that Jacques was sitting behind her desk at the head of the class. His hands were folded together in front of him, in much the same manner as when Klaas had found him in his workshop.

A gasp escaped Claira as her arms gave out, allowing the books to tumble to the dusty floor. She stood motionless, staring at Jacques with a great unease showing in her eyes.

Jacques smile at her. "My lady," he said in a friendly tone. "You have arrived. That is good. Many young minds to teach."

"Jacques....you...." But Claira could say no more. She put her hands over her mouth and was silent.

"Do not be afraid," Jacques said, his voice calm and almost soothing. Claira had never heard him sound this way before, and this fact increased her feeling of unease to fear. "I bring no fowl thought, nor harm to this room," Jacques continued. "I am at peace of the mind."

"Then why...." Claira whispered through he hands.

"Why am I here?" Jacques finished for her. "Well, that is simple, my lady. I am here for one last conversation before I leave. And, believe me when I tell you, this time I have something very interesting to say."

"Leave? Where are you..."

"Tut-tut," Jacques interjected. "All in good time." He gestured to the first row of student's desk. "First, come and sit. It is hard to exchange words with you loitering all the way back there."

When Claira showed no intention of moving, he said, "Come, come. I am not here to harm you. In fact, I am here to give you my blessing."

Claira frowned. "Your blessing?"

"Yes, yes, my blessing," he repeated. "To wed my brother. Now, please, come and sit up here. Let us converse this one last time."

Slowly Claira moved up to the front of the room.

"Good," Jacques encouraged her. "Now have a seat." He motioned to one of the small student's desk. "I would let you have your desk, but I fear my long legs would not fit into such a tiny space as those tables offer."

Claire sat down. Her knees rubbed against the bottom of the desk, but beyond that, she fit quite easily.

"There," Jacques confirmed. "That is much better. Now, as I said, I am here to give you my blessing. You and my brother, Klaas, should indeed marry tomorrow. I had a long chat with him yesterday morning at my factory, and he promised me that his intentions towards you are pure. He will make a fine husband, as I am sure you will make a fine wife."

"But Klaas told me that you and he quarreled yesterday," Claira said. "Is that not so?"

Jacques sighed. "Yes that is true. Unfortunately, the ease of conversation that you and I share is not comparable to that of myself and my brother. He can be judgmental and I, in turn, can be closed minded and stubborn." He smiled down at Claira with a condescending smirk. "I regret that it is a rare day when we can talk together and not have it become an argument. This saddens me and I wish it were not so. But, brothers will be brothers." The smirk remained on his face, belying the sincerity of his words.

Though she wanted his words to be truthful, Claira was still leery. "What is it that changed your mind?" she asked. "The last day we spoke, you were very upset by my announcement."

"And I still am," Jacques replied. "But what am I to do. If marrying my brother is what will make you happy, then that is all I can ask. Your happiness, not mine, is what matters here. But I do tell you this; I cannot stay in this village any longer. I am poised to leave this very evening." Either this was honesty or he was just a very convincing actor, Claira could not tell.

"Leave? Why must you leave?"

"As happy as I am for you, and even as happy as I am trying to be for Klaas, I cannot stay here and witness the love you share. It is too difficult for me. I may not have *deep* feeling, but I do have *some* feeling. I can hurt as can anyone."

Claira found herself beginning to feel sadness for Jacques. She attempted to extinguish it by remembering all of the disagreeable things he had said to her in their frequent conversations, but still she could not rid herself of this growing sense of pity for him. She said, "I thought you were to be King of this land?"

"One day I will be King," Jacques confirmed. "But not of this land."

"Then where will you go."

After contemplating this for a moment, Jacques said, "Perhaps I will seek out my father's homeland. Surely there will be a place for me there."

"I....." Claira had to clear her throat before she could continue. "I will miss our conversations."

"As will I, my lady." Jacques smiled again, then stood up. "Well, I must be off. Lots to do. Always lots and lots to do."

"Take care of yourself, Jacques."

Jacques came around the desk and looked down at the young maiden. "You, my lady, may call me Jack," he said. He pinched her cheek lightly, then stepped past and headed for the front door of the schoolhouse.

"Enjoy your wedding day," he called over his shoulder as he went. "I am sure every person in the entire village will be there to help you celebrate. It will be a glorious day indeed."

Then he was gone through the door, leaving Claira still sitting with her knees rubbing against the bottom of the small desk.

Wedding Eve

The night before the wedding, Claira and Klaas sat together on the front stoop of the toy factory, sipping hot cocoa and gazing up at the starry summer sky. Claire told her fiancé all about her strange confrontation with his brother at the schoolhouse. Klaas listened patiently and quietly, making no comments until she had relayed the whole story. Then he leaned back in his seat and continued to look up at the night sky, still with no comment.

The couple sat silently like this for a moment, until Claira grew impatient. "What are your thoughts, Klaas?" she asked. "Are his words true?"

Klaas sighed heavily. "I cannot be sure."

"But you were quite insistent that he possessed a good heart. Why do you doubt now?"

"I truly believe what I have said to you," Klaas confirmed. "However, I have never known my twin to expose a soft side or to be so open and gentle with his words."

"Perhaps he does harbor true feelings for me," Claira offered. "And spoke kindly as to not alarm me more than was necessary."

Klaas nodded. "This could be possible. But, I cannot deny a feeling that haunts me. It whispers in my mind that things are not as they seem. For Jacques to give up so easily and leave the village......It is all very odd and completely against his nature."

"He presented as quite sincere." Claire mused.

"I desperately want to believe that he was," Klaas agreed, running his fingers through his long brown beard. "It pains me to doubt my brother. And yet, if he does speak the truth, it upsets me that he feels his only option is to leave his home."

"Perhaps you should try to speak to him."

"No," Klaas said firmly. "He made it quite clear that I am to seek him out no further."

"Then what, Klaas?" Claira pleaded. "What is it you will do?"

Klaas smiled then and took his brides tiny hand in his own. He looked in to her beautiful green eyes. "Well, the first thing I am going to do is pledge my everlasting and truly eternal love to the woman of my dreams," He said. "I shall marry you in front of the entire village and will not think again of my brother until this important piece of business is done."

"I love you so much," Claira whispered, and kissed him on the cheek.

"What a celebration our love will be," Klaas said, looking again to the sky. "It shall be a grand and wondrous event for all."

And it truly was.

Wedding Day

The next morning, the entire village crowded around the small outdoor alter to witness these two lives as they promised their love to one another. Klaas wore a long crushed velvet jacket of red, tied at the waist with a white, silken sash and collared by fur. Claira dressed in a perfect white gown with sparkling jewels and beads painstakingly sewn onto the bodice. A lace veil fell over her face.

But Klaas would not have it. As soon as he stepped up to stand beside his bride, he gently lifted the veil off her face. "I shall never allow your beauty to be hidden, my love," he whispered to her.

After the ceremony, Klaas led his new wife into the village square. "I have a surprise for you," he told her as they walked hand in hand, with the crowd of happy villagers following close behind.

As they entered the square, Claira's eyes shone with delight when she saw what awaited them there. It was the most wonderful sleigh that she had ever seen. The entire body of this sleigh was covered with the same red velvet as Klaas' coat, and trimmed all around with the same white fur. Silver bells that adorned all the corners and rails shone with a shimmering intensity in the bright morning sun.

Even more incredible was the fact that this sleigh was not pulled by just two reindeer, as Klaas' old wagon had been, but eight. Each animal was dressed with finest leather halters and silver buckles. Bells also decorated their long, curved antlers. Claira smiled and pointed happily when the bells tinkled gently each time a reindeer moved its head.

As Klaas led her up to the sleigh, Claira gasped for she was sure that one of these reindeer turned and smiled at her.

"Shall we go for a ride, my wife," Klaas asked her.

"But Klaas," Claira said hesitantly. "There are no wheels. How will it travel over a ground that is not snow covered?"

"I have constructed the finest sleigh for you, my love," Klaas said, taking her hand to assist her up. "The skis are very special. They are designed to move over any surface, be it grass, gravel, or snow. And I'm sure you will find the movements much smoother than any rickety old wagon."

"It is wondrous," Claira said as she set herself down on the soft, fur lined seat. "Truly it is, Klaas!"

"A perfect sleigh ride for my perfect wife," Klaas mused as he sat down beside her and took the reins in his hands. "Now off we go!"

With one quick whistle and flick of the reins, the reindeer lurched forward.

The villagers cheered and chortled as the sleigh pulled away. Claira waved at them all happily and called out, "Begin the festivities without delay! We shall join you shortly!"

The eight strong animals pulled the sleigh across the rocky ground with great ease, and just as Klaas had said, the terrain of the land was little felt by the newlyweds.

They travelled over hills and across fields, and stopped by a sunny pond, where ducks swam and dove for food. They sat on the grass together and watched the water fowl for some time. They talked of their future together, but also just sat quietly, holding hands and enjoying the warmth of the day.

When they finally returned to the village, the square was beautifully decorated with streamers, tinsel, and flower blossoms of every imaginable color. The musical sounds of mandolins and fiddles sang through the air. People danced, laughter and high spirits swirled this way and that as though blown by a summer wind. Food and wine was plenty, and all was merry. It was a celebration beyond any that could be remembered. It continued through the day and into the evening, and still the festivities showed nary a sign of ending soon.

When only a sliver of sun remained visible on the horizon, Klaas' mother went to her son as he sat with his new bride. She hugged him tightly and said, "My heart is filled with joy for you Klaas."

Klaas looked into Nature's eyes and smiled. "I know, my kind mother. And yet I see sadness in your eyes that cannot be hidden by laughter and gaiety. What troubles you on this perfect day?"

"It is a perfect day," she agreed. "But for one thing. I cannot stop my heart from missing your brother. Jacques should be here sharing this joyous time with his family."

"Yes," Klaas said. "I am troubled by this also, but the choice was his to make. We must accept his decisions, regardless of the pain they may cause us."

"You are a good man," Nature said. Then she looked at Claira. "And you, my dear, complete him perfectly. What a lovely couple you two make."

Claira embraced her. "Thank you, Mother Nature. We are so glad you are here to celebrate this time with us."

76

"Yes," Nature said. "But now I must be off. My old bones are weary and my mind is tired. I will return home to my bed and rest."

"I will take you," Klaas offered.

Nature shook her head. "Do not be silly. I will not take you away from your bride on this day, even if for a moment. I have my faithful mare tethered just at the edge of the square. She will see me home safely."

"Very well," Klaas ceded reluctantly, knowing that any argument he made would fall upon deaf ears. "But ride slowly. Darkness is upon us."

"Fear not for me," Nature hugged her son anew. "For, as you recall," she whispered in his ear. "I am not as frail as I may seem."

Sometime later, Nature arrived home safely. After she had rubbed her horse down and given the animal a big armful of fresh smelling hay, she meandered slowly to the house and let herself inside.

As she closed the door behind her, Nature shivered. Despite the warmth of the day, the air of the little room she had entered was quite chilled. Though this did seem slightly odd, Nature was very tired and chose not to concern herself with it. She shrugged and continued to the kitchen table to retrieve a candle.

Once lit, the dim light of the taper jumped and move through the kitchen creating ghostly, animated shadows. Nature considered making herself a cup of tea to warm the chill out of her bones, but decided against it. The quilts on her bed would provide all the warmth she needed.

She followed the dancing glow of the candle into the bedroom and then set it down on the top of a clothes chest. Once more an icy shiver ran up her spine. Surprisingly, it was even colder in this room than it had been in the kitchen. So cold, in fact, that she could see her breath shimmering in the faint candle light. Nature's brow creased with confusion as she hugged her arms around herself. This was very odd.......

Suddenly Nature heard a shuffling sound behind her. Then, before she had a chance to wonder at the disturbance, a voice, low and eerie, floated out from the back of the room to greet her. "Hello mother."

She spun around and a gasp escaped from her lips. Jacques was standing only an arm's length away, staring at her with a twisted smile pulling at his thin lips. In her tired and surprised state, Nature thought for a moment that he looked taller than she remembered.

"Jacques," she breathed, feeling some relief that it was her son and not a strange intruder. "Klaas told me you had left. I am so hap-"

As Nature was about to move so she could embrace her son, she saw something in his eyes that made her stop. A feeling of dread washed over her, just as the ocean tide would crash over the sandy shore. She tried to step back, away from him, but her hips bumped against the chest behind her, causing the candle flame to sway back and forth, making the room seem as though it were ablaze in the swirling light and dark.

"Do I frighten you, mother?" Jacques asked. Nature found that the calm and steady sound of his voice only added to her feeling of dread.

"No......of course not," Nature said, trying to keep her tone as steady as his had been. "But why, my son, do you look at me in such a strange manner? As though you do not know your own mother?"

"Oh, I know you," Jacques replied, taking a small step closer to her. "You are Mother Nature, the all important keeper of the Gift of power."

Now Nature felt fear as well as dread. Jacques was staring at her with hatred showing clearly in his eyes. His hands twitched at the ends of his long arms and his smile was so wide that it was wonder his face did not crack wide open from the strain.

Yet, regardless of her unease, standing tall and brave, Nature faced her son. "This is becoming inane Jacques! Why are you here?" she demanded in a voice tingling with anger. "Just what is it you require of me?"

"Only to ask you a question," he replied.

"Then ask it so you can be gone. You seem quite not yourself and I am feeling unnerved by your presence."

"Unnerved are you," Jacques spat. "Am I not as endearing as your precious Klaas?"

Despite her growing fear, Nature frowned at him. "Do not speak to me as though I am not your mother," she said angrily. "For I believe I have garnered your respect, if nothing else. Ask your question and be gone from my house until you have again found your manners."

"I will ask it," he said. "First as a son would ask his mother. With kindness and love. And even, my dear, with that respect to which you place such importance. But I warn you, if you force me to ask my question a second time, it will be as a King asks his greatest enemy. With power and force."

As Nature stared into Jacques face, she realized with great sadness, that whatever part of this man that had once been her son was now gone. She no longer knew this person that stood before her. She hung her head, not able to look into the eyes of this stranger. "Ask your question and do as you will," she said, almost in a whisper.

Jacques face loomed over her, cracked and broken by the shadows of the flicking candle light. "Where is the box?"

The Gift of Power

At the wedding celebration, Klaas twirled his new bride around the dance area, with the band playing jolly tunes behind them. He took her under the arms and lifted her high into the air. Claira giggled and screamed with delight. Looking up at her, Klaas said, "I could never imagine loving anyone as much as you. You are......"

As his words trailed off, Claira could easily see the expression of Klaas' face turn from happiness and joy to dread, so quickly and extremely it was as though he possessed masks that could be change without notice. "What is it, my love?" She asked with sudden and deep concern. "What troubles you so suddenly?"

He mindlessly set his wife back to the ground. People around them continued to dance and move without regard to the change in their hosts. No one noticed as Klaas just stood, staring blankly at Claira.

"Klaas," she shouted as to be heard over the loud music. "What is it? What is wrong?"

Finally he looked into her eyes and Claira could see such terror that she felt an icy shiver claw its way up her spine.

"I am not sure...." He began, but his words were cut short by a tug at his coat tails. Turning, he saw that it was Sming standing just behind him. The elf's skin was pale and the look on his face mirrored the expression that had just overcome Klaas' own features. "Sming," Klaas gasped, kneeling before the tiny man. "What is it? Why are you here?

"It pains me greatly, Mister Kris," Sming said. "To disturb you on your greatest day of celebration, but we had nowhere else to go."

"We," Klaas echoed, looking around. "All of the elves are here?"

"The rest stay hidden just inside the forest line."

"What is it? Why have you left Jacques' factory?"

"I fear," Sming said, so softly that Klaas could almost not hear his words over the music. "That Sir Kringle has lost his senses. He raves like a mad man, shouting things that cannot be understood by my ears. He frightens us."

"Jacques? Are you speaking of my brother Jacques?"

The elf nodded his head slowly.

Klaas could not understand. "But Jacques left the village last night."

Sming shook his head. "No, Mister Kris. He was still at the factory as the sun was just setting on this day. He broke many things in his rage. And he called for us over and over, but we would not come out of our hiding. We were fearful that he may want to break us as well. We crept out only after he had gone. It was a long wait, for he raved on for much time. So many things......that made no sense."

"What things?" Klaas asked desperately. "What was he raving?"

"His destiny. Many times about his destiny. And a gift. He called it out again and again. His destiny is a gift? Or the gift is his destiny? I could not understand. It made no sense, Mister Kris. His mind has left him."

"No," Klaas said, mostly to himself. He stood back up again. "I believe his mind is exactly where he wants it to be."

Immediately Claira was behind him. "Klaas, what is it? What is going on?"

Klaas ignored her for just a moment. "Sming," he compelled the elf. "Go to the forest and gather the rest of your people. Lead them all to my toy factory. Stay inside. Do not come out. Do you understand?"

"Yes, Mister Kris, yes," the old elf said. "But why? Do you know what has happened with Sir Kringle?"

"There is no time," Klaas shouted at him. "You must go now! Do not delay another moment! Get your people to the factory!"

Sming rushed off with the double step, hop, hop, method of hurrying unique to elves. At any other time Klaas would have noted it with amusement, but now he only turned to his wife. He took her face in his hands and kissed her.

"Klaas, what is it," Claira asked again. "What...."

But Klaas stopped her. "I am afraid," he said. "That I have failed you, my love. You and the people of this village, and of this land. I have made a grave mistake."

"Klaas...."

He silenced her with another kiss. A long kiss, as though it was to be their last. When he finally drew away, he said, "I need you to do something, Claira."

"Yes, anything," she said.

"You must tell all of these people to go home. Tell them that right this very minute they are to go home and lock their doors and windows. They should not leave their homes, no matter what happens. This is a desperate time. You must make them all understand. *A desperate time!* Can you do that my dear? Can you make them understand?"

"Yes, of course. But why…."

"We have not a second left to spare, Claira. I wish I could turn back the clocks and change the decisions I have made, but I cannot. You must act quickly. After these people have dispersed, you shall go without haste, to the toy factory. The elves will be there…. stay with them. I will come for you there."

"But where are you going," Claira pleaded. "Please do not leave me."

"The choice is not mine, my love, for if I do not go, surely all will be lost. Now, please, do as I have told you. I will meet you at the toy factory."

Then, before Claira could say anymore, Klaas turned and ran off towards the sleigh he had so lovingly built for his new bride.

"Please be swift, my friends," Klaas called to the reindeer as he jumped aboard the sleigh. "For I dread that the worst may have happened."

Before he had even picked up the reins, the reindeer shot forward and within seconds they were speeding through the streets of the village.

Klaas' first thought was to seek Jacques out at his factory, but he quickly realized that would be an error. His brother wanted the Gift. The Gift was at Mother Nature's farm. So that was where Jacques would be.

As the sleigh sped through the village, gray storm clouds began to roll in over the land as quickly as sand through an hour glass. Thunder rumbled in the darkening sky and a heavy rain began to fall, drenching the village. Within moments, torrents of mini rivers crashed down the streets.

Klaas shook the reins. "Faster my friends," he yelled, as bolts of lightning broke across the dark sky. "Though we may already be too late!"

When the sleigh finally stopped in front of the Kringle farm, the rain was falling so hard that Klaas could barely see the little house that was his mother's. He jumped down and immediately slipped in the wet soil that was beneath his feet. Straightening himself again, he ran for the house, his boots erupting through large, black puddles as he went.

Klaas threw open the front door of the Kringle home and ducked inside. The kitchen was dark and quiet and eerily chilled.

"Mother," he called, moving through the kitchen towards the back rooms. He almost tripped over a stool that was all but invisible in the darkness, just managing to keep his footing.

Nature's bedroom door was closed, but Klaas noticed a dim flicker of light peeking through the crack at the floor.

"Mother," he called again and burst into the room.

He saw Nature lying on her bed on top of the quilts. She was still fully clothed with her arms folded across her chest. Her eyes were closed.

"Mother," Klaas gasped and rushed to her side. "Mother, wake up!" He reached down and touched her pale face. Her skin was ice cold. "No, mother, please!" He cried, sitting down on the bed and pulling the woman in his arms. "Please, you must wake up!" He rocked her back and forth. "Please wake up! I need you!" But to no avail, his mother remained still and silent.

"How good of you to come." These words floated out from the back of the bedroom as though they were carried by a whispering breeze. Klaas twisted around and saw his brother standing over a small table. A candle flickered there, and beside it was the Gift. The colorful ribbons and cloth paper had already been removed, and Klaas could easily recognize the wooden box he had constructed for his father so many years ago. It was still closed, but Jacques' thin fingers were caressing the lid. "Now," he continued, "I will not have to seek you out."

"Jacques," Klaas breathed. "What have you done to mother?"

"She forced me to ask twice," he replied. "I warned her and yet she still resisted." An evil smile twisted at his lips. "And you all said that I was the stubborn one."

Klaas carefully laid Nature back onto the bed, then stood up. Rain water still dripped from his beard and hair as he took a slow step towards Jacques. "Why are you doing this, Jacques?" he asked.

"Do not call me that," Jacques snapped. "That name is dead to me. My name is Jack."

Klaas took another step forward. "You have hurt our mother, Jacques," he replied, refusing to acknowledge his brother's new name choice. "Why would you do that? She is a kind and gentle woman. She is your mother!"

"She was a liar!" Jacques yelled at him. His fingers continued to drum on the lid of the box. "She and father both were liars and thieves!"

"Thieves? Nothing has been stolen from you!" Klaas shouted, as rage began to vibrate through his body. "Your selfish greed has deceived your mind!"

"Father possessed the power inside this box," Jacques said. "And then convinced us it was evil so he could prevent me from inheriting what is rightfully mine! I will rule this magic even better than he did!"

"A piece of whatever dwells inside that box killed our father," Klaas reminded him. "Do you not remember his warning? If the Gift is used in any other way than what was instructed, the punishment will be an evil beyond any reckoning! Look out the window, brother! See how the weather is changing simply because you are touching the box! Use your mind and imagine what will happen if you open it!"

Jacques placed both of his hands on the edges of the lid. "I care not about the weather!" he told his brother. "I shall do with the weather as I please once I have claimed what belongs to me! This power was created for me and I will command it!"

Klaas moved again towards Jacques. "I know there is good in your heart, Jacques," he said, trying to calm his voice. "I beg you, please. Seek it out now and let it show you how wrong this is."

Jacques threw back his head and laughed. It was a high pitched and piercing cackle that cut through the air of the room like a knife. "Oh, Klaas," He growled. "You are so naive. When will you grow up? You continuously trust your heart, though it lets you down time and time again. There is no good inside me. My heart is a frozen block of ice and the blood in my veins is venom. I say the things you want to hear and you believe. What a child you are."

"But I do not believe you now," Klaas stated, preparing to jump at his brother.

But, just before he was able to launch himself, Jacques screamed at him, "Then believe this!" And threw open the lid of the box.

A brilliant, blinding light exploded from inside the box and engulfed Jacques' entire body. This burst was so powerful that it threw Klaas all the way back, across the room. His back slammed against the wall hard enough to push all the breath from his lungs and he crumpled to the floor, gasping for air. Suddenly the room was rumbling and quaking as if the whole of the house rode atop an angry, bucking horse. Trinkets and glassware fell from shelves and a tall, highboy chest toppled over with a dreadful crash. The bed where Nature lay was bumping and jumping like it had come alive. Klaas grabbed onto whatever he could and forced himself to his knees. He looked back towards were Jacques had been standing.

What Klaas saw then was truly beyond comprehension. Only Jacques' silhouette could be seen through the magnificent white light that radiated from the box. His arms were stretched out and his hands still gripped the lid. His entire body pulsated and twisted. The opaque shadow of Jacques bulged and ripple with each convulsion, contorting in ways that were unbelievably inhuman. He was also growing taller by the moment, stretching up towards the ceiling of the room, until his head struck, forcing his shoulders to hunch forward.

Then, from inside the light, Jacques screamed. It was a screeching sound that split through the room and stung at Klaas' ears. He screamed again and again. Horrifying, animalistic shrieks like none that had ever been heard on the earth before.

Klaas clapped his hands over his ears and stumbled to his feet. The room still shook violently, but somehow he managed to keep his footing. With a shout of desperation, he threw himself towards the table where his brother stood. Immediately he felt the power of the box pushing back against him, as though the magic sensed his intent. He fought it with all his strength and slowly began to drag himself forward. At last his body tore through the force and as he fell into the light, his brother continued to scream and convulse. Striking the table with his upper body, Klaas brought both of his hands up and using every ounce of energy that remained within him, he slammed down onto the lid of the box, forcing it closed.

Just as it snapped shut, another bolt of power shot forth from the Gift, sending both Klaas and Jacques flying backwards. They struck the floor on opposite sides of the room and then each brother lay motionless.

The powerful light vanished the moment the lid was closed and the room became still once again. Outside the little house, however, turmoil continued to pound its vengeful fists upon the land. The stormy sky was alive with flashes of lightning, each strike followed instantly by a boom of thunder so loud it rumbled the earth. A frigid and icy rain poured down and was blown into swirling sheets by a heavy gale that screamed as it billowed through the village. Snow and sleet fell from the sky, mixing with the rain to form a thick fog of gray and white that whipped and twisted its ghostly way across the deserted square where, only hours before, people had been dancing in celebration.

Even far out across the oceans the water boiled with waves as high as trees. Below the surface, the sea floor cracked and rumbled as giant slabs of rock were pushed up through the waters until they erupted out of the rolling sea. One after another the huge mountains of stone collided with each other above the ocean's surface, creating new land masses that rose high into the sky. This happened all over the world, dividing the ocean, as an angry planet sought revenge for promises broken.

At the northern and southern poles, the coldest points of the earth, ice that had laid dormant for thousands of years was now split opened and shattered by the rage of the boiling ocean beneath. Gigantic shards of shimmering ice and snow were driven up into the sky. Some stayed, pushed high above the sea like massive, sparkling, blue mountains. But some of these blocks of frozen tundra cracked under their own immense weight and crashed down atop one another, creating sharp cliffs and frozen valleys throughout these new wintery lands.

From the ashes of a great betrayal, a new world was being born.

Jack Frost

Klaas opened his eyes and stared up at the ceiling of the bedroom. He felt dizzy and disorientated and for a moment could not remember where he was or how he had gotten there. Then he heard the storm that roared beyond the window of the room, and the memory of all that had happened came flooding back into his mind so quickly and painfully that he thought his brain might burst. He tried to sit up, but his body did not respond. He tried again desperately, but still he could do no more than lift his head. He could not move his arms or his legs at all. Though his head thumped with pain, he realized with a foreboding dread that beyond that, he could feel nothing.

This cannot be true, he told himself, and again tried to move. Still his body would not react.

Frantically Klaas glanced around the room. Without the light of the now extinguished candle, the bedroom should have been in total darkness, but the constant bursts of lightning that flashed outside the window illuminated the area with flickering clarity. He was flat on his back beside the bed where he could only hope that his mother still lay. The rest of the bedroom was in total chaos; furniture was tipped over, pictures had fallen from the wall, and broken glass was scattered all around. Klaas could see that the Gift still sat atop the small table, which had miraculously not toppled over or fallen. He felt just a moment of relief when he saw the lid of the box was closed. But then the image of his brother's twisting and contorting silhouette tore into his mind, driving home new shards of pain behind his eyes. All at once, fear clawed away any feelings of relief he had enjoyed so briefly. On the verge of panic now, Klaas scanned the room further, trying to spot any signs that Jacques was still present. At first, from his low vantage point, he could not see anything but broken furniture. Then he spotted something through the inconsistent pulses of light. It was an unrecognizable shape; no more than a large, lumpy mass pushed up against the wall opposite to where he lay. His eyes were watering badly, so he squinted, trying desperately to get a better look at whatever was crumpled there. Finally he noticed something else, the inanimate, oddly shaped lump appeared to be moving. Slowly and rhythmically, up and down.

Breathing.

"Jacques," Klaas called out. His throat was dry and his voice sounded hoarse and uneven. "Jacques! Brother, is that you?"

Now the thing began to move more, seemingly in an attempt to straighten up. Despite the rumbling thunder that roared outside, Klaas was quite sure he could hear its labored breath. And, as he listened more closely, he could hear something else as well. A strange sound, snapping and popping, as though its bones were no more than dried twigs, breaking with each little movement it made.

Klaas could feel his fear growing. He tried again to move, but from the neck down, his once strong body was useless and still.

He considered calling out again, still grasping at the hope that it was only his brother, possibly injured and struggling to stand. But as the figure straightened up more, and Klaas was able to see its form better, he realized with horror that whatever it was; it definitely did not resemble Jacques. It rose higher and higher, until its head touched the ceiling. Yet still it continued to rise, forcing itself to hunch its neck, then its shoulders and back. The creature was not facing Klaas, so he was only seeing it from behind. In the sporadic flashes of light that punched violently through the window, he was now able to make out the monster more clearly. Though it appeared to be clothed in a shiny blue colored jacket and trousers, both garments were much too short for its incredibly long, thin limbs; as if a father were trying to wear his child's clothes. The exposed skin covering its skeletal frame was blue. A pale, icy blue liken to a clear sky on a crisp and chilled autumn morning. Just under this seemingly transparent surface, darker blue veins spider webbed all around like zig-zagging cracks.

As Klaas continued his pointless attempt at movement, a sudden and piercing crackle of laughter erupted from the blue figure. The sound sliced through the small space of the room like a dagger and bore bolts of pain into Klaas' ears. He yelled out, but was unable to hear even his own screams over this immense and terrifying cackle.

93

Then, just as suddenly as this horrific noise began, it morphed into words. "Oh, brother," it screeched. "What a conundrum we are in!"

Klaas' breath stopped in his lungs. Shock clouded over his mind and he had to shake his head to stay coherent. Though he knew that this thing could be mocking him by calling out 'Brother', there was something familiar about its voice. Under the high pitched, gravelly tone, it sounded like Jacques.

"Jacques?" Klaas asked, and then clamped his mouth shut. He had not intended to speak at all, but the word had somehow pushed its way past his lips. It was as if by saying his brother's name, then his brother this beast became.

The blue thing began to turn then, dragging its head and hunched shoulders across the ceiling. Its spine creaked and crackled as it moved, like the sound of ice on a frozen pond breaking apart under the rays of a new spring sun.

"Your brother," the thing croaked as its face came into view. "Has perished. His heart is but a frozen lump of ice within my chest. What stands before you now is Jack Frost." With these words, Jack Frost took a lumbering step towards where Klaas lay. The wooden floor board under its gnarled foot immediately froze, then crystallized and splintered.

Its face was colored the same pale blue as its limbs, but a thick layer of frost on its long cheeks and forehead shimmered in the flickering light. A small beard of icicles dripped down from its pointed chin. Long, glistening icicles of hair also hung from its head, jutting out this way and that in all directions. And, as the thing looked down at Klaas, its purple-blue lips peeled back into a hideous grin. Rows of razor sharp ice shards sparkled inside its mouth as a grotesque blue tongue darted out suddenly and flicked at the tip of its twisted nose.

But as Jack Frost moved closer to him, it was the frozen beast's eyes that horrified Klaas more than anything else. For in each bulging, silvery- blue orb, he could easily make out the ghostly image of his brother, trapped for an eternity, his mouth frozen into a terrified scream that could no longer be heard but would never end.

"Jacques," Klaas murmured. His fear was forgotten as a black cloak of despair closed in around him. "What have we done to you, my brother?"

"Pity," Jack Frost snarled. "You have the nerve to feel pity for your brother! You are the one that made him what I am. You lied to him. You stole from him. And now, Klaas Kringle, you shall suffer for him."

With that, the beast raised its long, knobby hand. Its stick-thin fingers were the length of a child's arm and each was capped with a sharp, icy claw that glinted and glistened as they moved slowly above Klaas.

Sudden Klaas felt a great tightness around his chest, as though he were entwined in the coils of a giant snake. He gasped for breath, but the power of Jack Frost would allow none to find his lungs.

Jack Frost twitched his fingers again, and then Klaas was being lifted off the floor. Another twitch, and he continued to rise until his face was mere inches from the vile creatures flickering blue tongue.

"Before this is finished," the beast hissed, now so close to Klaas that frozen bits of spittle from its mouth stung his face like tiny bees. "I want to make you a promise."

"Promise me nothing," Klaas said through laboring breathes. "And get on with your business, for the smell of your breath repulses me."

Jack Frost cackled at this, its tongue twisting and slithering behind its frozen teeth. "A joke for all occasions," it said. "That is exactly why the people loved you so."

"Do what needs to be done," Klaas shouted. "I care not to spend another moment with you."

"Soon," the thing chortled. "Very soon I shall remove your heart from your chest and watch with joy as it freezes in my icy grip. Then, and this is my promise to you…Kringle," it growled. "I will do the same to Mother Nature who rests so peacefully. And after her heart is but snow on the floor, I will leave this house and find our love, Claira…"

"How dare you speak of her!" Klass roared, as loudly as his constricted lungs would allow. "You fowl beast! Simply by uttering her name with your grotesque mouth you have defiled her loveliness!"

"Oh, oh," Jack Frost mussed as its grin widened, tearing even deeper into its ice covered cheeks. "That struck a nerve." It chuckled happily, rocking its frozen head against the ceiling. "But let us not be too hasty. Perhaps I will not harm our love. Instead I will keep her close. Even take her as my wife. A wife who will stand by my side as I turn this nasty village into a block of ice. She can watch while I cast my icy power across the oceans, freezing every wave and ripple until they can move no more. And she will witness my strength and marvel at my power as I create a planet that is nothing but a frozen, desolate waste land."

Klaas wanted to yell. He wanted to scream his anger into this things face. Jack Frost had stolen his brother from him! And his Mother! And now it wanted his love and his people! He longed to curse it, sending it back to whatever chilled and terrifying nightmare it had come from. But he could find no voice. Nothing was left in his lungs but a long, agonizing moan.

Jack Frost chuckled again. "How does it feel?" it asked, bringing its face so close to Klaas that its twisted nose touched his forehead. "Tell me how it feels to have all that matters to you stolen away. How does it feel to finally have someone you can hate?"

Klaas looked into Jack Frost's budging, blue eyes. The image of his brother remained there, frozen forever in a silent scream. "I do not hate you, Jacques," he whispered with his last, desperate breath. "I pity you."

The grin on the beast's face disappeared as rage flowed through it. Jack Frost roared. "And now your pity can die with you," it snapped, bringing its hand down towards Klaas' chest. "Die with the knowledge that what was once fleetingly yours is now mine for an eternity." Its ice covered claws pushed against Klaas' paralyzed body. "And that I shall enjoy wearing your heart as an icy charm around my neck."

The moment its needle sharp claws cut through his clothes and touched his chest, Klaas' skin began to freeze. As they pierced his flesh, a vein of frosty ice darted up his neck and into his chin and cheeks, instantly freezing his long beard to a snowy white. Klaas moaned as Jack Frost's icy venom climbed further up his face towards his eyes.

Then suddenly there was a great flash of yellow light from where the Gift still sat. It instantly filled the room with brilliance and warmth.

A booming voice echoed out of the light. "Step away from my son you demon of ice!"

Jack Frost snarled and jerked its head around. It snarled again as it saw the glowing image of Noel Kringle, standing with his right hand resting atop the Gift of Power.

"You have done enough damage here," Noel commanded. "It ends now!"

Though Jack Frost merely cackled at these words, it did pull its claws away from Klaas, sending the consuming frost into retreat. "You are but a specter," It rasped. "The specter of a man who was weak in life. I have no fear of you! There is no power left in this world that can harm me!"

"You have betrayed forces that are beyond your reckoning," Noel warned the beast that had once been his son. "And now it is time for you to suffer the consequences of that betrayal."

With that, Noel brought his left hand up. He splayed his fingers wide and released a bolt of white power that stuck Jack Frost squarely and then held him tight. The beast squealed in surprise as the invisible grip it used to ensnare its victim failed. Klaas fell back to the floor but remained still.

Noel jerked his hand sideways, and immediately Jack Frost was dragged into the center of the room.

The beast roared with rage and a sudden terror. It tried to leap towards Noel, but the force that entrapped it held strong. "Release me old man!" it screamed. "Or I shall freeze you even beyond death!"

"Your greed has doomed us all, Jacques!" Noel bellowed. "Everyone will now suffer because of what you have done!"

"Everyone will surely suffer if you do not release this hold on me!" Jack Frost growled. "This I promise you!"

"You shall make no more promises or create anymore lies. I will tell you this; I made a vow so long ago, with the earth and the water and the sky. It was a vow to help the people of this land! But now it has been broken! Because of your selfishness and ignorance, we have enraged this planet that supports us!"

"I need no support!" it screamed. "I am Jack Frost! I am all power over all things!"

"Your evil greed still deceives you, my son." Noel said. "There is no good in you. And where there is no good, there is nothing! You wish to rule over a land.....mighty Jack Frost? Then rule you shall! The forces of nature banish you to the southern pole. There you can rule over a desolate tundra of snow and ice for all of eternity. If you attempt to leave or if even one ounce of warmth touches you, your heart will melt, ridding this world of you forever."

"NO!" Jack Frost screeched. "I shall rule all lands!! No power can stop me!"

"Be gone now, my son," Noel said with a great sadness now softening in his tone. "We shall look to find you no longer."

Then, the window behind Noel crashed open with a loud thump, and a spiraling wind howled into the room. It whipped and moved about with power enough to lift even the toppled furniture off the floor. But this hand of nature found its target quickly. And, though the beast screamed and struggled with all its might, the tornado quickly engulfed Jack Frost and began to drag it towards the window.

"I will have my revenge," it shouted from within the circling mass. "I promise all, I will have my revenge!"

The monster continued to thrash violently, desperately grabbing at anything in the room that might give it some purchase. But everything it touched instantly turned to ice and shattered within its frigid grip. Finally, with one last tug, the wind sucked the vile creature, which had once been a Kringle, out the window and Jack Frost disappeared into the stormy sky.

Noel Kringle

Klaas open his eyes and stared into the tiny bedroom. He could no longer hear the storm raging outside and noticed that some of the furniture which had once been toppled was now standing upright again. And the Gift of Power no longer sat on the tiny table.

Panicked, Klaas jerked his head around and saw his father sitting on the bed were Nature remained in her ghostly slumber. The box, which was again wrapped in the colorful cloth paper, rested on his lap.

"Father," Klaas gasped. "Father, help me, for I cannot move."

Noel looked at his son and frowned. "That is odd," he said calmly. "For your body contains muscle, and tendon, and bone, all the things necessary for movement. That is very odd indeed."

"I speak the truth," Klaas pleaded, not understanding his father's callousness. "I can...." And then he realized that he could move. Whatever force it was that had held him immobile was now gone. He got to his feet with ease.

"There," Noel mussed. "That was not hard, was it?"

Klaas looked down at himself, lifted one foot and shook it about, as though needing further proof that all was well. Then, with a sudden and shocking start, he realized that he was in the presence of his long deceased parent.

"Father," Klaas breathed, looking up with amazement showing his eyes. "How can you be here? You took your leave of this world so many years ago."

"Yes," the old man agreed. "But I also promised that if you were ever in need, I would be here. And you were most certainly in need, so here I am, as promised."

"But father...." And then Klaas saw his mother lying motionless on the bed beside Noel. Despair once again folded over him as he moved towards her. "Mother," he cried. "Jacques has slain my Mother Nature."

"Slain?" Noel echoed the word as though it had no meaning to him. He looked down at his wife. "She is not slain. She merely rests." He leaned over then and kissed her on the cheek. "Wake up, my love. There are things to be done."

Nature's eyes fluttered once and then opened. "Noel," she said softly and smiled at her husband. "How wonderful to see you."

"And how wonderful it is to be seen by my beautiful Nature," he replied.

Klaas was so filled with joy that even the astonishment he felt no longer mattered to him. "Mother, I was so afraid..." He sighed and hugged her tightly in his arms.

"I told you long ago," Noel said. "That as long as the Gift existed, then so would the Kringles. And here sits the Gift, safe and sound." He patted the top of the box gently.

But Klaas' happiness did not last for more than mere seconds as the memories of all that had happened began to play back through his mind. He turned and walked slowly to the window. Outside, dawn was just breaking over the horizon. For as far as his eye could see, the ground was a chilly, sparkling white. Fat snowflakes continued to float down from the gray sky, although the wind that had whipped it into such a fury earlier had now ceased to blow.

"It is winter outside," Klaas said, staring out at the cold landscape. "And yet, is it still not the summer months?"

"Yes," Noel confirmed. "Great damage has been done here this night."

"It is my fault," Klaas said as he turned to face Noel and Nature again. "I have failed every task that you bestowed upon me."

"Klaas, no….." Nature began to say, but Noel raised his hand to stop her.

"We have all failed," he said. "We all wanted so desperately for there to be good in Jacques, that we blinded ourselves to the truth. From the moment he was born, the evil that is greed was alone within his mind. This poison was all that drove him. Our son was a lost soul." Noel looked to his wife and saw tears welling in her blue eyes. "We can cry for him now, my dear," he continued and touched her cheek. "But we must never forget what he has become. Our hearts shall be closed to Jack Frost forever more."

Nature put her hands over her face and wept.

"What will happen now," Klaas asked.

"We are to be punished for our failures," Noel replied sadly. "Just as your brother has been punished. It pains me greatly to tell you this, and yet I must. You are banished from this land forever, my son. And you must go now, of your own accord. If you delay, I am afraid that the force that took Jack Frost will..." He paused and glanced away from his son to stare at the bedroom window, which was once again closed. When he looked back, there was a rare sign of fear showing in his eyes.

Klaas nodded slowly and acceptingly. "I understand," he said. "But what of these people? They are in need of me now more than ever before. These times will be difficult for them."

"They are strong," Noel stated confidently. "They have endured many hardships before this and have survived. They will surely survive these times as well. I will take Mother Nature with me when I go, as she is also a Kringle and cannot stay in these lands any longer. We shall journey high into the mountains with The Gift. There we can live peacefully among the trees and the animals. And we shall continue to open the Gift each year. I am hopeful that in time, Mother Nature and I, and the power that still remains in the Gift, may be able to undo all that has happened here this day."

"But where am I to go, father," Klaas asked. "This is the only home I know."

"You will go as far away from Jack Frost as is possible, for he is even more crafty than your brother. If he ever finds a way to escape his prison of ice, he will spare no energy in seeking you out."

"Where," Klaas asked again.

"The North Pole," Noel told him. "It is icy and cold and secluded. No one will ever venture there. There you will be hidden from all eyes. Perhaps you can build a new toy factory, even grander than the first."

"What good are toys," Klaas murmured sadly. "For I shall be alone in a dungeon of ice."

"Grieve not, my son, for a gift I have for you. Once a year, on the same day that the Gift of Seasons is to be opened by Mother Nature, you shall be free to travel where ever you please throughout the world. You can deliver your toys to the children of all lands. But hear me; as the sun rises on the next day, you must return without haste, to the North Pole."

"Thank you father," Klaas said and hugged the old man. "For believing in me."

"Yes, yes," Noel said and patted his son's back. "But you must also believe in yourself. Now kiss your mother and then you should be off. You cannot stay here for much longer."

Still rubbing the last tears from her eyes, Nature hugged her son. "One day," she whispered in his ear. "We shall meet again."

Before Klaas exited the room, he asked Noel one last question. "How, father, am I to get to the North Pole?"

Noel smiled. "There is magic in you, my son. I can feel it. It must have leapt inside you as you struggled to close the box."

"But I feel no different," Klaas replied, touching his chest as though the magic where something he could sense with his fingertips.

"It is like me," Noel said. "When you need it, it will be there. You may use it as you must. But always remember to guard yourself from the bad. It lurks everywhere. You are a gentle man, so it is easy for you to see good, but you must also teach yourself to see the bad. This is the best advice I can give you."

"Thank you father," Klaas said again. "Thank you Mother Nature."

Then, with no more delay, he left the room.

Klaas and Claira

Outside the house, Klaas found that the snow was as deep as his knees. He looked around, but could see nothing but white.

Then he thought for a moment, of what Noel had said. 'There is magic inside you'. This seemed so strange because, as he had told his father, other than the pain in his chest were Jack Frost had held him, he felt no different than before. Klaas wondered, *if there is truly magic inside me, would I not feel at least something, even if it is only a small difference.*

As he contemplated this, standing knee deep in the snow, he heard a sound coming from the barn. It was a thumping sound, as though many hammers were striking the ground at the same time.

Klaas turned this way and began to fight his way through the snow. It was slow and exhausting, and his feet felt frozen inside his boots, but eventually he made it to the barn.

He threw open the doors and saw a wondrous sight. Eight reindeer, all stamping their hooves against the barn floor. And they were still harnessed to the sleigh that he had built for his love.

"My friends," Klaas exclaimed. "You waited for me. What intelligent and amazing animals you all are."

Continuing to stomp their hooves, the reindeer all huffed and chortled with anxious excitement.

"Yes, you are right," Klaas agreed. "We must be off."

He jumped aboard the sleigh and grabbed the reins in his hands.

"As speedy as you are able, my dear friends," Klaas shouted. "To the toy factory!"

Over the slippery snow, the sleigh traveled very quickly indeed. After what seemed like mere seconds, the reindeer stopped in front of Klaas' factory. He leapt over the snow and onto the front stoop, then burst through the door.

Claira was immediately in his arms.

"Oh Klaas," she cried. "I have been so worried. All that has happened. The storm, the snow. I feared the worst. I am so happy you are finally here."

Klaas hugged her tightly. "I am here my love."

Claira looked into his face and he saw sudden surprise light up in her eyes. "What has happened to your beard," she asked.

Klaas was confused. "What do you mean?"

"It is as white as the snow that falls outside," she told him.

He touched his beard casually and said, "It is a very long story that will have to be told at another time. First, I need to ask you a question. The most important question I will ever ask."

Claira expression changed back to worry and concern. "What Klaas? What is it?"

"I can no longer stay here," he said. "I must leave the village at once."

"Klaas," Claira exclaimed. "Why...."

"I ask you, my love," Klaas continued, interrupting his wife's upset words. "To come with me. I know that you care for the people here and I will understand if you choose to stay and help them in their time of need. We are wed, and I want to spend every moment of my life with you, but I also know you are a kind hearted and caring woman. I shall hold no ill will if you feel you must stay. So, now I ask again. Will you come with me?"

Claira looked into her husband's eyes and replied, "If you were to ask this question a thousand times, each time my answer would be the same. Yes. Yes and yes and yes, I will come with you."

"My love," Klaas murmured and hugged her again.

"Where is it we will go?" Claira asked when they drew apart.

"Far, far away, to the North Pole." he said and took her hand. "And we must go now."

But Claira resisted. When Klaas turned and looked at her questioningly, she said, "What about the elves?"

"The elves?" Klaas echoed, and then, for the first time since he had entered the room, he saw them. At least fifty or sixty tiny men, women, and children all crowded into a huddle around the pot belly stove. They were looking at Klaas with their small, nervous eyes.

"They have nowhere to go," Claira continued. "For they lived so long inside Jacques's factory that their home is now gone. We cannot just leave them here."

"Then we shall not," Klaas announced. "They will come with us."

All the elves cheered and rushed over to encircle the couple. "Oh, Mister Kris," Sming, the oldest elf, said. "We knew you would not abandon us. You are the kindest of men."

"I thank you all," Klaas said as he pushed his way through the crowd of happy elves. He turned then and faced them. "But we really must leave. Right this moment and without any further delay."

Still cheering and shouting, the elves rushed for the door.

On the front stoop, everyone stopped and looked curiously at Klaas' sleigh. The reindeer gazed back at them with matched curiosity.

Claira stepped up beside her husband. "Your sleigh is wonderful and lovely, Klaas," she said. "But I fear there is not enough room for even half of these elves."

"Do not despair, my love," Klaas said confidently. He touched his finger to the side of his warm, red nose. "For I believe it has much more room then it may appear." Then he called out to the elves, "Everyone hop aboard!"

One after another, the small people jumped into the back of the sleigh, each finding just as much room as the one before. In moments all of the elves were peeking happily over the edge of the sleigh.

Claira's eyes were wide and surprised. "How did you do that?" she asked Klaas as they took their seats up front.

He smiled at her under his white beard. "You are in for many surprises," he said and flicked the reins. The reindeer leapt forward, dragging the filled sleigh easily through the snow.

As they travelled faster and faster Claira seemed worried. "Should I not go to my house for some things? I have no more than the wedding gown that I am wearing."

Klaas smiled at her. "And how lovely you look in it," he said. "But, fear not, my love and trust in me. I shall provide you with all you need."

Faster the sleigh went, gliding smoothly over the frozen terrain. Soon the Great Mountains appeared before them. But still, they did not slow.

"Klaas," Claira exclaimed with fear showing in her eyes. "We must stop now! Surely you do not think we can travel over those mountains in a reindeer drawn sleigh!"

Klaas flicked the reins again. The reindeer reacted and sped up even more.

"Klaas, please," Claira whimpered. "I am frightened!"

Klaas put his arm around his wife and pulled her closer to him. "Trust me, my sweet Claira," he said a second time. "For I will always keep you safe."

As the Great Mountains loomed before them, Klaas flicked the reins one last time and again laid his finger against his nose. "And away we go!" he called out in a jolly, excited voice.

Suddenly the reindeer's hooves were no longer pounding against the hard packed snow, but kicking through thin air. They were climbing into the sky, as though they now ran along an invisible road that travelled to the stars. The sleigh bumped once, and then followed them into the snowy air.

Claira screamed as they shot higher and higher into sky. Up and up, over the Great Mountains, and still they went higher, gliding through the wind, swooping and turning.

"Take us higher, my friends," Klaas shouted and laughed a rolling, jolly laugh. With every kick of the reindeer's legs, they rose farther into the open air. "Look Claira, look at this view!"

Slowly she pulled her face out from where it had been buried under Klaas' arm. The wind grabbed her golden hair and tossed it this way and that. It felt so crisp and exhilarating against her face that Claira could not help but start laughing herself. "This is amazing," she called out to her husband, and then laughed more.

The elves cheered and giggled behind the couple. "Higher, Mister Kris," Sming hollered. "We have never felt so tall!"

So up they went. Klaas' booming laughter echoed through the sky, "Ho Ho Ho," as they sped forward, towards their new home in the snow.

"Oh, Klaas," Claira called, hugging her husband again. "You are an amazing man!"

"No," he said to her. "I am just a man. No more, no less."

Then they were gone. But the adventure was just beginning.

The End

Taylor stared up at her father with wide, astonished eyes. "That's it?" she asked with amazed disbelief in her tone.

Joe smiled as he stood up and began to tuck the bed covers around his daughter. "That's it," he confirmed.

"But that can't be it," Taylor argued, though she did it through a large and tired yawn. "There's so much more I want to know. Did Santa....I mean Klaas, make it to the North Pole ok? And how did he build a toy factory if there's nothing but snow and ice? And how did Jack Frost escape? I mean he must have, right? You said he breathed ice onto my window. Is he out there now, still looking for his brother?"

Joe leaned over and kissed her on the forehead. "Sounds like someone might be starting to believe."

"I never said that I didn't," Taylor replied fervently. "Please dad, tell me what happens."

Joe shook his head. "Not now. You promised that if I told you this story that you'd go right to sleep. You don't want Santa to think you were fibbing, do you? Because fibbing is bad and he'll know."

Taylor sighed sleepily. "No." she said. "I guess not."

"Good," Joe mussed. He kissed her again before turning to leave the room. "Now, right to sleep. Tomorrow is a big day."

"Dad," Taylor called just as Joe was reaching to turn off the bedroom light. He paused and looked at his daughter.

"Yes, Tazie?" he said reluctantly.

"How did Klaas become Santa Claus?" she asked.

Joe smiled again. "That is a question for another time," he replied. "And another story." Then he turned out the light and quietly left the room.

Maple Ridge, BC
September, 2014

Made in the USA
Charleston, SC
23 September 2014